Praise for the Aggie Mundeen Mystery Series

RIVER CITY DEAD (#4)

"San Antonian Nancy G. West delivers a tantalizing tale about murder, mystery and mischief in River City Dead. Set against the backdrop of San Antonio's vibrant Fiesta Week, River City Dead features an appropriately colorful protagonist, Aggie Mundeen. Determination has a tendency to get Aggie in trouble, especially when it's coupled with her penchant for playing amateur sleuth. Here, Aggie has her mind on other things—namely, romance—having planned a River City rendezvous with the man she loves, SAPD Detective Sam Vanderhoven, at a hotel on the San Antonio River Walk. What could go wrong? Turns out there's nothing that puts a chill on hot romance quite like cold-blooded murder." *-The Katy News*

"This well-written cozy mystery is easy to follow with its fast-paced narrative. River City Dead is peppered with humor, wit, and a nice touch of romance. The Texas setting and use of Fiesta Week as backdrop give distinctive flavor to this novel. Highly recomended."

\- *Mystery Tribune*

SMART, BUT DEAD (#3)

" *Smart, But Dead* is the perfect combination of brains and heart. A tight mystery, an irrepressible heroine, and superb writing."

– James W. Ziskin, Award-winning author

SMART, BUT DEAD (#3)

"Will keep you guessing until the last page. Well-written and excellent storyline. Highly recommended!"   – Obsessed Book Reviews

DANG HEAR DEAD (#2)

"Well-paced and written, there are bursts of humour in this novel which had me roaring with laughter. The plot is intricate with a satisfying ending. ...A great read and highly recommeded."
    – Diana Hockley, Australian Mystery Novelist and Reviewer

"Suspenseful, engaging, funny, and unique. I loved following Aggie as she asked questions and followed clues. You will fall in love with Nancy G. West's writing, just as I have."   *-Universal Creativity Reviews*

FIT TO BE DEAD (#1)

"*Fit to Be Dead* has it all: intriguing characters that point to romance, an engrossing plot, a compelling puzzle and well-disguised clues—a fun read."   – L. C. Hayden
Award-Winning Author of the Harry Bronson Mystery Series

"Aggie Mundeen's wry observations on life, death, and the struggle to whip mind and body into shape make *Fit to Be Dead* delightful. Joining a health club has never been so dangerous...or so amusing."

    – Karen McCullough, *Shadow of a Doubt* and *A Question of Fir*

RIVER
CITY
DEAD

**The Aggie Mundeen Mystery Series
by Nancy G. West**

FIT TO BE DEAD (#1)
DANG NEAR DEAD (#2)
SMART, BUT DEAD (#3)
RIVER CITY DEAD (#4)

Psychological suspense
NINE DAYS TO EVIL

Aggie Mundeen Lake Mystery #(1)
THE PLUNGE
A novella

RIVER CITY DEAD

An Aggie Mundeen Mystery

Nancy G. West

RIVER CITY DEAD
An Aggie Mundeen Mystery

First Edition
Trade paperback edition | January 2017

Second paperback edition | January 2022

This is a work of fiction. Any references to historical events, real people, or real locales are used fictitiously. Other names, characters, places, and incidents are the product of the author's imagination, and any resemblance to actual events or locales or persons, living or dead, is entirely coincidental.

Trade Paperback ISBN-13: 979-8-9851369-2-0

Southwest Publications

Printed in the United States of America

ACKNOWLEDGMENTS

As a native San Antonian, I delight in our unique River Walk with its festivals and flavors. But without input from the wonderful people below, this book wouldn't exist. I am grateful for their knowledge, help, time and support.

- Author/historian: Lewis F. Fisher
- Battle of Flowers Association: Carol Canty, Lauren Cothren, Sue McClane, Jane McFarlane, Lynn and Thad Ziegler
- Casa Rio Mexican Food: Elaine Glasscock Olivier
- City of San Antonio: Joseph Cruz, Lincoln George, Kelly Kapaun, Devon Lambert, Christine Morgan
- Ft. Sam Houston National Cemetery: Frank Farris
- ISS Grounds Control: Roger Hastings
- Metal Plating: Corky Phipps
- Trinity University Professor/Chemist: Joseph B. Lambert
- San Antonio hotels: Brian Getman, Michelle Flores, Marissa Torres
- Shops at La Villita: Angelita, Casa Manos Alegres, Equinox, River Art Group, Starving Artist Art Group benefiting Little Church of La Villita, Villita Stained Glass
- Texas Cavaliers: Phil Bakke

I'm forever grateful to Donald R. West, who supports my compulsion to write, even when it interferes with a normal life.

Any errors that exist in the novel are mine.

I do not, however, accept responsibility for whatever Aggie Mundeen might do.

One

April 1998

Not every city has a river running through it. And not many women plan a rendezvous at a San Antonio River Walk hotel during Fiesta Week after years of self-imposed celibacy. I was about to make history.

Sam and I were meeting at Casa Prima Hotel. Hopefully our first days and nights together in River City would be more fiesta than fiasco.

And we could avoid dealing with crime.

To calm the jumping beans in my stomach, I decided to make a quick detour to Barnes and Noble. Instead of turning south from Hildebrand toward downtown, I turned north on Highway 281 and headed toward Loop 410. If SAPD called Sam away, I'd need something to read. He assured me they wouldn't contact him, but sometimes they had to rely on an experienced homicide detective for a difficult case.

Barnes and Noble was packed. After a lengthy search through half the store, I found aisles brimming with romance novels. I didn't relish being caught scouring this area. In my *Flash-News* column, "Stay Young with Aggie," I answered readers' questions about everything from fitness to relationships. As an "expert," I wasn't supposed to need help.

It wasn't as though I was innocent. I became painfully experienced after Lester the Louse seduced me when I was barely eighteen, impregnated me and vanished like mist. But stories of other people's romances might be enlightening.

Slipping down an unoccupied aisle, I reached for a title that caught my eye, *A Well-Spent Night*. A bare-chested, muscled Scottish hunk wearing a plaid kilt bulged from the cover. I squinted at the title, which upon closer inspection actually read, *A Well-Spent Knight*. Worked either way. I flipped pages to the middle, found what I was looking for and started reading. There was a lot of heavy breathing and rippling biceps, but it never said why the guy wore a kilt or how he got it off. I'd wondered about that. Historical romance might not be the thing.

I replaced the book and continued down the aisle. The face-out cover of *Steaming in Hawaii* gleamed with electric blue ocean water and swaying palm trees. A gorgeous half-dressed couple grasped each other beside the cobalt ocean. Sam and I would have a swimming pool at our River Walk hotel. Close enough. I slipped the novel off the shelf and flipped through pages. The title did not refer to steam from Hawaii's volcanoes. Skimming pages, I noticed contemporary novels offered details and felt my body parts tingling.

From the corner of my eye, I saw a young sales girl eyeing me. Was my face flushing?

"Can I help you?" About twenty-five with swinging hair and a pouty mouth, she looked sexy, bored, and all-knowing.

Whipping the novel under the arm laden with my shoulder purse, I reached blindly toward the shelf for another novel, hoping I didn't look like a waif grasping for crumbs.

"So many choices." I doused her with my superior bank-teller expression. "I doubt if any of these books are really that good." Another cover caught my eye with the title *The Long Hard Ride*. A shirtless muscle-bound cowboy stood spread-legged front and center while a steer romped around behind him. I snatched the book off the shelf.

"Imagine that," I said. "You even have westerns." She smirked. Some urge compelled me to jabber. "I don't think he could ride a steer dressed like that."

The new-fangled phone jangled in my purse. I resented the impertinent metal box demanding my attention. Digging to retrieve it, I dropped the books. The sales girl swiveled over and scooped them up. "I'll keep these at the counter while you search for more." She cocked a corner of her sulky mouth before walking away. I fumbled to flip open my Motorola StarTrac.

"Where are you?" It was Sam, using his professional detective voice.

"I just needed a few things. Have you seen the...our room?"

"You need to get down here, Aggie. We have problems. I'll meet you in the lobby." He hung up.

That was the last thing I wanted to hear. Scouting the quickest route to the exit to avoid the sales girl, I skirted through rows of books, sailed out into the sunshine and headed for my Wagoneer. I rolled down the windows, leaned my head back on the seat and inhaled clean April air, convincing myself that whatever problem Sam encountered couldn't be that bad.

Revived, I cranked up Albatross, my station wagon, headed south on 281 and turned right on McCullough toward Broadway, the main thoroughfare to downtown and the Fiesta parade route. Huge paper flowers with streaming ribbons decorated doors. Shop windows proclaimed "VIVA FIESTA!"

Crews were setting up roadside bleachers for several hundred thousand people to watch parades later this week. Civic-minded ladies organized the first parade to honor President Polk's visit, stopping horse-drawn carriages in front of the president's viewing stand to lay wreaths in front of the Alamo, the shrine of Texas' independence. Resuming their parade, they threw flower petals at onlookers, creating the Battle of Flowers Parade in 1891, the first Fiesta event.

How perfect that Sam Vanderhoven and I would begin blending our lives during Fiesta. At least that's what I hoped we were doing. Since he was an SAPD Homicide Detective, I naturally tried to impress him with my investigate skills. Unfortunately, my headstrong (he might say, "irrational") behavior frustrated him. The last time I intervened against his advice, I almost got myself killed. At least the crisis made us realize we loved each other. We'd even pledged to trust one another, which might prove to be the bigger hurdle.

The towering Casa Prima Hotel loomed in the next block, re-activating my jumping beans. What did Sam's call mean? Had he discovered a crime, considered the burden of my pesky interference and decided to jettison our rendezvous?

Two

Sam

The hotel manager notified SAPD Detective Sam Vanderhoven that a woman might be dead in the penthouse.

"Since I think she's dead," the manager said, "I was reluctant to call EMS and have them screeching up here in the middle of Fiesta Week. I thought you could handle it."

"I'll go right up," Sam said. "We have to notify EMS, but I'll tell our dispatcher to have them douse the sirens and use the service elevator."

Sam radioed SAPD's dispatcher to notify EMS and advise the Patrol Sergeant of a possible suspicious death. The sergeant would send patrol officers. He took the elevator to Casa Prima Hotel's penthouse.

The man in the perfectly tailored suit standing outside the suite looked deathly pale in contrast to his red power tie. Sam walked toward him, hand extended. "Sam Vanderhoven, SAPD. EMS is on the way."

"Hotel Manager Harry Haddock. I'm pretty sure she's dead. I can't believe this is happening during Fiesta. Did you ask EMS to come through the back entrance to the hotel?"

"Yes. When did you find her?"

"The maid, Sara Giles, found her in the room and called me about ten minutes ago. I came right up, looked in the suite and asked Sara to sit over there." He pointed to a table and chairs at the end of the hall.

"We'll talk to her. Did you see anybody else on the floor?"

"No."

"Have you talked to other guests?"

"No."

"Okay. You stay here. I'll have a look."

Sam walked into the room and saw her. There was no blood or signs of trauma, but her chest didn't rise and fall from breathing. Wrapping two fingers in a single layer of his handkerchief, he placed them on her carotid artery and didn't feel a pulse. She could have died of some unknown physical malfunction, a drug overdose or murder. He didn't think she'd been dead long. He studied the position of her body.

He took a quick walk through the entire suite—living room, bedroom and bathroom—conducting his preliminary investigation. Studying details, he was careful not to disturb anything that might be evidence. He saw drag marks in the carpet from the bathroom, through the bedroom to the living room. It looked like one person's shoe prints dragging another person to the sofa. Once he documented everything he could see with the naked eye, he knew the death was suspicious and called Homicide.

"Louis, this is Officer 3856 at Casa Prima River Walk Hotel. I was in the lobby waiting to meet somebody and got a call from the manager saying there was a seriously ill, possibly dead girl in a penthouse suite. I had the dispatcher call EMS. There's no trauma or bleeding, but I think she's dead. She's late twenties to early thirties, and carpet indentations show two sets of footprints, as though somebody dragged her to the sofa. Her body looks like somebody positioned it. Who's on duty?"

"Rick Montaya is next up."

"I just started my RDs, but I can hold this down until he gets here. I can stay on as backup."

"Good. I'll tell the Patrol Sergeant we're sending Rick."

"Thanks. We'll need several officers. The manager is worried about publicity ruining his business."

"Got it. Montaya is on his way."

Rick Montaya was an energetic, capable detective. Sam let out a sigh and went back to view the victim. Tragic. Unbelievably tragic.

Using the same footpath he used before, he walked back to the manager standing in the hall.

"Did you know the victim?"

He nodded. "Monica Peters. She was a guest every year during Fiesta Week."

"Does anything in the room look out of place to you?"

Haddock reluctantly peered inside the room. "No. Neat and clean as usual. Except for..." He cleared his throat and blanched.

"I understand. Did the maid comment about the victim or the room?"

"When she called, she said she thought the woman in suite three might be dead. When I came up, she was crying and pointed to the body."

"I see. Why don't you go stand down there in front of the penthouse lounge. An officer will come talk with you."

Walking to the other end of the hall, he introduced himself to the maid who found the girl, asked a few questions and instructed her to stick around so an officer could take her statement.

He was back in front of the elevators when Detective Rick Montaya stepped off.

"Rick, I'm glad you were next up. I just started my RDs and came down here to meet a special woman...first time we'll have a weekend together. Good timing, huh? I can stick around as backup. The girl is down there. Come see what you think."

Rick followed him into the room. Both remained quiet as Rick studied the victim and absorbed the scene. He pointed to drag marks in the carpet. Sam nodded. Both men followed the marks with their eyes back to where the woman lay.

"Yep," Rick said. "Suspicious." He lowered his voice. "She could have been doing drugs with a friend and overdosed. Maybe he dragged her around trying to revive her. When he couldn't, he panicked and fled. Did the manager see anybody around?"

"No one except for the maid who found her. She's waiting down the hall for an officer. Here's my notes on what she said. I don't think the victim has been dead long. I considered broadcasting a BOLO, but it would have led to a thousand questions from every officer around wanting to know who to be on the lookout for and the basis for detaining them. Plus, it would put the killer on alert, if there was one. We can't be sure what happened."

"We may not know until the autopsy." Rick shook his head. "She's young. Pretty. Lots of crazies out there. I think it looks suspicious enough that Patrol will call Evidence."

"I think so too. EMS is coming in through the back. The manager is worried his hotel could be ruined for Fiesta Week."

The Patrol Sergeant stepped off the elevator with three officers. He and Rick identified themselves, and Rick caught them up to speed. Patrol Sergeant Spears stationed Officer Valerie Garrett at the elevator door to stop anyone unofficial from entering or leaving the floor and maintain an entry log of persons coming and going. He instructed the other officers to take statements from the maid and Manager Harry Haddock.

Rick turned to Sam. "Don't you need to meet somebody?"

"Yeah. Thanks, Rick. I'll be back." When the elevator opened, the EMS crew clattered off rolling their stretcher. He pointed them to the scene, spoke to Officer Valerie Garrett and stepped inside. EMS would do everything they could to revive the girl, but he thought it was too late.

Just before he pushed the button, he had an idea. He went back to the penthouse lounge and peered in. Officers were writing reports and Haddock was standing to leave.

He spoke to one of the officers. "If you're finished, I need to talk to Mr. Haddock."

"Sure. I'm done."

Sam drew close to Harry Haddock. "You should check the phone log for calls coming in and out of the victim's room." Harry nodded. "Detective Montaya will probably remind you." He talked to the manager a while longer in low tones, headed for the elevator, stepped inside and pushed the button to the lobby.

Whatever else was happening in his life, as a law officer, crime tracked him like an insidious nasty aroma. After two years dealing with Aggie's dogged determination to "help" him investigate, and his constant attempts to keep her out of trouble, he was finally meeting her at this hotel. Despite conflicts, they admitted they loved one another. He understood her motivation to solve crimes. He shared it. They planned this romantic rendezvous for months. No doubts. No fear. No crime.

Now this. She probably had her hair done, shopped for Fiesta clothes and packed every bright outfit she owned. She'd be miserably disappointed. After she got over the shock, she'd want to help him. Since the crime occurred in the suite they were supposed to have, she'd probably be more determined than ever to find the person who hurt this girl. He had to make sure Aggie didn't land in danger investigating without making her feel like he was brushing her off.

Three

Albatross and I approached the entrance to the hotel's underground parking garage. A sign said the garage was full. Once my eyes adjusted to the dugout's dark interior, I recognized the top of an EMS van. What was going on? Was Sam in trouble? Injured?

Swallowing my fear, I eased my car up to the main entrance and asked the valet to park my car. Not knowing what to expect, I asked the bellboy to put my luggage by the registration desk. Neither man looked rattled by some catastrophic event, but they looked down their noses at Albatross. I hadn't owned many cars, so I named them. Albatross was my long-time companion.

I entered the lobby in my hot-pink tank top and swishy skirt and looked around. My espadrilles, multi-colored canvas with rope wedges, were a Fiesta staple. My toes, painted to match my tank top, peeped out. A nice touch. Where the tile met a rug, I stumbled. The heels on the espadrilles were pretty high. I recovered and straightened my shoulders.

At the other end of the lobby, past the restaurant and bar, I saw a garden-like setting with palm trees and a blue sky beyond, the hotel's entrance to the River Walk. The tinkle of happy chatter tickled my ears. I could hardly wait to get out there. I knew Sam had some sort of problem, but I was too excited about Fiesta Week to believe it could be anything insurmountable.

I sashayed toward the check-in desk drawn by the fragrance of gardenias.

Miniature trees on either side of the desk, protected by clear plastic shields so nobody could touch the petals, were strategically placed to intoxicate guests.

A large sign to the left of registration read, "Welcome Fabulous Femmes!" I smiled. Off to the sides of the main traffic area, in offshoots from the lobby, police officers spoke with two women. One was slim and chic, dressed in beige linen. The Hermès scarf that wrapped around her neck and flew down her back must have cost a fortune. The splash of silk in bright Fiesta colors was the perfect accessory. What wouldn't I give to be tall, slim and chic? I could exercise and eat tofu until hell froze over and it wouldn't happen.

The other woman wore a striped sheath in multi-colored neon as intense as the first woman's attire was subdued. Her smile was even brighter. Maybe they were two of the Fabulous Femmes the hotel welcomed on the sign. I wondered why police were talking to them. Maybe officers were allowed to flirt during Fiesta Week.

Sam would be in civilian clothes. I looked around, didn't see him and approached the check-in desk where the bellboy had placed my luggage. "I'm checking in later, but could you store this luggage for me?" The clerk asked my name, came outside the desk to tag my suitcase and handed me a claim ticket.

"I'm looking for—"

"Aggie. Over here."

Sam stepped off the elevator. He wore a shirt with sleeves that stopped just above muscular arms. His collar lay open with curly chest hair peeping out above a very flat stomach. I blinked away images of the kilt and the cowboy and opened my eyes to see Sam's brown ones looking into mine through his horn-rimmed glasses. An unruly shock of hair flipped crazily over his forehead, but his face was serious. He took my arm and led me toward a sitting area. "I'm afraid things have drastically changed."

I looked him up and down. He didn't appear injured, but his expression was unusually serious. "What is it? What's wrong?"

"A crime was committed in the penthouse suite reserved for us."

"What kind of crime?"

"A young woman is dead. It looks suspicious. It's possible she was murdered."

My knees started to buckle. He took my arm to steady me and eased me into a chair.

"She's dead in our room?"

"I'm afraid so." His features softened. "I didn't expect to get a penthouse suite, but the assistant manager called me early this morning, said the occupant was scheduled to vacate, and the suite would be ready this afternoon. The maid found her about half an hour ago." He studied my reaction. "Are you okay?"

I nodded. Blood must have been returning to my head.

"Why don't you sit here a few minutes. I need to get back up there. I'll know more when I come down."

"Okay." As he headed for the elevator, I sank back into the chair. What were the odds somebody would die in our hotel during Fiesta Week? That some poor woman would lose her life? In our room?

Sam would be preoccupied with this crime. Our rendezvous had been kicked to the back burner. Another room nearby would be hard to find during Fiesta Week. After he returned to relay the details, I might as well go home. I could watch the parades on television and keep in touch with him by phone. I sighed.

Despite our differences, Sam and I had grown steadily closer. He still grew apoplectic when I helped investigate a crime and landed in danger.

He'd explained his reticence to marry and never mentioned it again. But I knew he loved me. We were here. Finally. We deserved this long weekend. He was the right man. Whatever we had to face, we could face it together.

I stood, squared my shoulders, walked to the elevator, stepped inside and pushed the button to the penthouse.

When the door opened, a female SAPD officer stood there with a set jaw, a determined face and a clipboard. Shiny auburn hair framed her striking face. Even clothed in the ill-fitting police uniform, she curved in the right places.

"Can I help you, miss?" She emphasized "miss." With her eyes darting around under thick lashes, she appraised me like a livestock judge.

She blocked my entrance to the corridor. I planted my feet.

"I'm with Detective Sam Vanderhoven. Our room is up here. He said there's a problem and for me to come up."

Her eyebrows peaked. "Sam wouldn't say that. This is a suspicious death. Civilians aren't allowed."

"Why don't you ask Detective Vanderhoven?" I moved to step around her.

She blocked me and raised her voice. "I don't have to ask anybody."

Sam must have heard her. He stepped from a room down the hall and strode toward us. "What's the problem, Valerie?"

"This woman says she's with you and you told her to come up here."

"I see." He looked at me over his spectacles. "This is Officer Valerie Garrett, Aggie. One of SAPD's finest. Valerie, this is Agatha Mundeen, a private investigator I sometimes consult."

"Hmmp." Officer Garrett stepped aside with a look on her face that could curdle cream.

I gave her my sweetest smile. There should be a law against police departments hiring attractive women. These men worked such long hours. Away from their families. If they had families. I touched the bare finger of my left hand.

Sam took my elbow and steered me down the hotel corridor swarming with police. He spoke quietly. "They told guests the hotel cordoned off the penthouse to resolve a maintenance problem. Valerie, Officer Garrett, is instructed not to admit anyone to the floor."

"I see."

He dropped the professional expression. "You shouldn't be up here, Aggie. I asked you to wait in the lobby."

"I wanted to be with you. I can at least see the suite we were supposed to have."

He stopped. "There's a body in there. We're handling it as a crime scene. You can't enter the room."

At one end of the hall, police talked to a well-dressed, middle-aged couple. Near the other end, officers walked in and out of the last suite where yellow and black crime scene tape dangled from the door. Left of the suite, at the other end of the hall, a double door looked like the entrance to a lounge. When I glanced back, Valerie Garrett was watching. I took a step toward the suite with the dangling yellow tape. "I could just peek in."

He closed his eyes and took a deep breath. Before he opened them, I made it almost to the door. Before I got there, Sam caught up and clinched my arm. "It's a young woman. Much too young to die. Are you sure you want to see this?"

"Yes."

We reached the threshold. I peered inside and jerked in a breath. In the center of a beige, ultra-suede sofa, a beautiful young woman lay draped with her head on a bright pillow. She held another pillow to her chest. The life had drained out of her. I knew her.

Four

I stared at her and swallowed the bile in my throat.

"You recognize her," Sam said.

"I'm afraid it's Grace's daughter-in-law, Monica Peters. The three of us had lunch together last week."

"I'm sorry, Aggie. The manager told me her name, but I didn't make the connection with Grace."

I couldn't take my eyes off the girl, so vibrant only a week before. Small-boned and delicate, she looked childlike in death. With light accentuating her pretty features, she looked like an angel with makeup. I'd been with her only once, and her face was partially turned away, but I was almost certain it was Monica. Soft rays streaming through a skylight spotlighted her as though Heaven had opened to shine notice that this young woman should not have died.

The EMS team had pronounced her dead and were packing up their gear.

"That's Detective Montaya." Sam pointed to a plainclothes officer. "He'll take the lead on this case."

Officers who must be SAPD's evidence team swarmed the room. I had to look fast before Sam decided to sweep me away from the scene.

In the suite that would have been ours, pieces of stout Mexican furniture stood at focal points on the periphery. Airy glass-topped tables seemed to float near upholstered pieces.

Delicate pastel colors of ecru, white, and teal decorated furniture and drapes. Tall vases of heavy Mexican hammered silver, strategically placed, held bursts of paper flowers in fuchsia, yellow, purple and orange, providing stark contrast to the pastels. Eclectic décor echoed the city of contrasts. Sofa pillows were fuchsia and orange. The hotel probably rotated pillows and flowers in the soft-toned room to suit the seasons, reserving the brightest colors for Fiesta.

When the evidence photographer used a flash, I saw metal shining on the table and on the front of her dress.

I squinted. "Are those pins?"

"Fiesta medals. Organizations make them and people collect them every year to pin on their clothes." A police officer picked up the medals with a gloved hand and bagged them for evidence.

To the right side of the suite's living room, a door opened to the bedroom we would have shared. A pale beige comforter ribboned in white lay over a massive four-poster king bed. Creme, tan and white petals splashed across the center of the comforter. Plush pillow covers, soft beige trimmed with white, leaned against the headboard. Purple, fuchsia, and orange accent pillows lay tossed in front.

The suite must have cost a fortune during Fiesta Week. My eyes filled. Sam gripped my arm and steered me farther down the hall. "Not exactly what we planned, is it?" He piloted me toward the penthouse lounge. "Let's go sit in there."

I glanced back and saw Officer Valerie Garrett interviewing an attractive couple at the other end of the corridor. Another officer midway down the hall talked with a young woman in a maid's uniform. "Did you tell the other officers why I'm here?"

"That's not their concern. They have a suspicious death to worry about."

He led me into the lounge, guided me to the nearest sofa,

handed me a glass of water and sat beside me. We had the room to ourselves.

"Do you know what happened to her?"

"Not yet. There's no blood, no obvious signs of struggle and no signs of forced entry. The maid, Sara Giles, came to check the room and found the body. We got the victim's ID from her purse. Headquarters is running a check on her."

"Did you find a murder weapon?"

"No."

"Why do you think she was murdered?"

"She's young. Dead of no apparent cause. Could be an undetected medical problem or drug overdose, but we haven't found any signs of it. The autopsy will verify the cause and manner of death."

They were always performed with unexplained deaths. I shuddered imagining it. He was back in detective mode. Efficient. Matter-of-fact. "From her driver's license, Headquarters will verify her identity and notify her next of kin. I'm sorry, Aggie."

I closed my eyes and pictured Grace getting the news. When a tear squeezed out, he pressed my hand. His phone rang. He jumped up, flipped it open and walked to the far edge of the room to answer. He listened intently, hung up and stood still a few minutes. Then he turned and walked toward me with a rigid face.

"They confirmed her identity." I stared at him. "The girl is Monica Peters. We have to notify Grace. There's an officer on the way to her house."

I'd been trying to process how some monster could murder Monica. Now pain closed around my heart and squeezed like I knew it would squeeze Grace's heart.

"I need to see her." When I stood, my legs wobbled and I sank back to the sofa.

"Sit here a minute. I'll check the crime scene and radio the officer going to Grace's. I'll tell him who you are and that you're on your way over. You can tell me later what you know about Monica. It may help us find her killer."

I felt numb.

He stopped at the door and turned back. "Aggie, it's possible guests will leave because of the murder, and another penthouse suite will become available. I talked to the manager about it. If that doesn't happen, he has a couple of small utility bedrooms staff members use when they have to stay overnight or become ill. They're more like cubbyholes than rooms. They're on two separate floors. He says we can use those." He waited.

I didn't respond.

"I know you're not thinking about this now, but I wanted you to know." He walked out of the lounge.

To comfort Grace, I had to regain control. She was nearly sixty-one and had lost three husbands. How much more could she stand?

I would send the valet for my car and drive to her house. I might claim my luggage from the front desk, go home to my bungalow next door to Grace's house and stay there. Sam was trying to comfort me about another room, but surely murder squelched his romantic inclinations. I was too worried about Grace to feel much of anything. It was doubtful we'd get a penthouse suite anyway.

In the corridor, I found him talking with Valerie.

"All but one couple in the penthouse has been cleared," she said, pointing to the couple at the end of the hall. "I'm just about finished with them. We advised them not to leave the hotel and asked them to stay in the lobby or restaurant. I'll go there when we're through."

"Good," Sam said. "I'll come down later and you can fill me in." Valerie gave me a smug look and walked toward the couple.

He turned to me. "We're bringing staff up here individually to get information for more thorough background checks, and to determine who was seen in the penthouse or has access. We have to make sure the hotel is safe for those who stay."

I sensed his mind was clicking through plans.

"We'll check entries, exits, fire escapes, windows and roof access. We'll contact local pharmacies and hospitals to see if drugs were stolen lately. Evidence took her purse. Any pills in the suite or her purse can lead us to her physician."

"That could take a while," I said.

"Yes, it will. I'm better off staying here. Aggie, since you're going to see Grace, maybe you should stay home. I can come to your house when I get sick of this place and give you an update. We can meet downtown for our weekend later. With a mob of people circulating around here and a lot of them drinking, River Walk hotels are on alert for possible violence. With this murder and cops swarming around in plainclothes trying to be discreet, it's not going to be a very festive atmosphere."

Sam would meet with Valerie, and he wanted me to leave. She would help him and the other detective solve this crime. He and I probably wouldn't have a suite, but at least we had a place to rest in the hotel's utility bedrooms, if it came to that.

"Right now, I'm going to try and comfort Grace," I said, glancing in Valerie's direction. "I'll be back."

He walked me to the elevator and held the door. The young woman they had interviewed walked toward the elevator.

"I'll keep you posted," Sam said.

"Same here."

Five

Stepping into the elevator, I dredged up a smile for the young, pretty maid who followed me in. She wore a perfectly pressed uniform and polished white shoes. Her expertly-cut hair shone, but she looked spent.

"Hello. I'm Aggie Mundeen."

"Sara Giles."

"I understand you found the poor dead girl. That must have been dreadful."

She nodded. "It was."

"How did you happen to find her?"

She breathed an exhausted sigh. "You're a friend of the police?"

"I help Detective Vanderhoven sometimes with his investigations." It was a stretch, but I liked the sound of it. "Detective Sam and I will discuss everything about the case. I'm considering getting a PI license. Whatever you say, I'll repeat it only to him." Most of what I said was true.

"Then I guess it's okay to tell you what I told the officers. I'm in charge of the penthouse suites, but I was reluctant to go to Monica Peters' room because she has lots of visitors. I saw two men enter and leave yesterday."

"Did you describe them to the officers?"

"I tried, but they were so ordinary. They were average

height and wore Jimmy caps, short-sleeved shirts, slacks or jeans and tennis shoes like hundreds of other tourists I see every day."

"Do they have video cameras in the penthouse corridor?"

"They have them on all floors in various locations. I haven't paid attention to where they are."

"You went to her room to clean?"

"No, I cleaned and vacuumed the suites this morning. I guess she was out having breakfast. I realized later I hadn't checked the bathroom bulbs, so I had to go back."

"The bulbs?"

"The hotel remodeled about a year ago. The city offered rebates for installing solar panels and skylights, so the hotel installed tunnel skylights in the penthouse bathrooms. They look exactly like ceiling fixtures, so you forget they're there. The skylights provide plenty of light in the daytime. But at night, the bathrooms are dark unless you remember to put bulbs in every single ceiling fixture."

"Tunnel skylights look the same as light fixtures?"

"Yes. They have glass or plastic convex lenses held by metal or plastic trims around them that are flush with the ceiling. For recessed lights, above the lens and trim is a housing for the recessed bulb. If it's a skylight, it looks the same on the ceiling, but the housing is a tunnel that goes up to a solar panel on the roof with a plastic or glass cover where the light comes through."

"I see. So you were taking bulbs to her room?"

"Yes. I listened at the door and didn't hear anything, but I hesitated to go in. I knocked, but there was no answer. I finally used my key to enter and saw her lying on the sofa. I knew she didn't look right. I feared she was dead, felt sick and screamed."

"Then what?"

"I called the manager. He came right away and called the police. He asked security to seal off access to the penthouse, tell penthouse guests there'd been a problem in one of the suites and ask them to remain in their rooms."

"How many penthouse suites are there?"

"Only six. They're pretty big. And there's a lounge for guests at the end of the hall. Penthouse guests and people from a couple floors below can use it."

"I was in there. It's lovely. Did you know the victim, Monica Peters?"

"I met her with a group of Fabulous Femmes, the ladies holding the convention. She was in the same sub-group I was in. After I started working here, I'd see her during Fiesta."

Two couples entered the elevator on the third floor. I couldn't ask Sara any more about Monica's death, so I changed the subject.

"I saw the lobby sign welcoming the Fabulous Femmes. Who are they?"

"They're a group of women who joined together to have fun and travel. They started here in San Antonio as the Foxy Fixits. They were primarily women who'd been active in social groups, were tired of volunteering and wanted to pick their own philanthropic projects."

The two women in the foursome smiled at each other knowingly.

"The San Antonio group took in other groups but kept their original Foxy Fixit name and concentrated on one charitable project a year. They reached out to other small groups of women because they wanted a big enough membership to get good discounts when they travel. They named the overall group The Fabulous Femmes. Now the Femmes extend nationwide."

"Does the overall group have a purpose?"

"At this year's convention, the Femmes are supposed to discuss whether to support some nationwide philanthropic venture or maintain their individual projects. My guess is that each sub-group will keep supporting pet projects in their local areas and join the Fabulous Femmes for fun and travel. Each sub-group is pretty distinctive, like the Flamboyants and the Madhatters."

Before I had a chance to learn more about the Femmes, the elevator stopped, the foursome left and Sara stepped into the lobby after them.

"Let's visit later," I called to her.

"Sure." She walked away.

Six

Sam

Detective Sam Vanderhoven went back to the scene and stood at the door. Monica Peters had been removed from the suite by people from the medical examiner's office. He could see carpet indentions from stretcher wheels and shoe marks of the EMS technicians who tried to save her. They had pushed their stretcher around the other end of the sofa from where somebody dragged her to it.

Rick came over. "Evidence photographed her and sketched the scene," he said. "They got several photos of the rug marks where it looked like somebody dragged the victim. He apparently covered his shoes, but we didn't see any fibers. Evidence agreed to do a zone search, separating the bathroom, two halves of the living room and the bedroom into zones where they dusted for prints. I explained it was a suspicious death and it looked like somebody tried to wipe prints from the surfaces, so they conducted an alternate-light-source sweep through each zone to fluoresce evidence not viewable to the eye: fingerprints, bodily fluids, hairs, fibers, glass and metal fragments.

"I even convinced them to use a trace evidence vacuum on furniture and rugs in each zone while I took notes. I had them work outward from the crime scene into the hall. I hope we'll learn if the girl was raped or detect traces of drugs or other lethal substances or unusual fragments or fibers. Maybe we'll get something. I wanted them to do the other suites, stairwell and rooms and the hall on the floor below, but I wasn't successful. We found her purse and ID. She's twenty-nine. We found a couple hundred dollars and credit cards. One card matches the number on her hotel registration. We're checking to see if the card was used after her death. From her driver's license, we learned she didn't leave her car in the parking lot. I'll go to her house later to see if it's there."

"You're real thorough, Rick. It turns out the woman I'm dating knew Monica Peters and is fond of her aunt. About the shoe cover marks on the carpet, we can estimate a shoe size but not weight and height, right?"

"Right. I just hope we come up with something. I had officers ask staff if they saw anyone hurriedly leaving the lobby. They also checked nearby businesses. Nothing. The ME investigator checked the body for lividity, trauma and wounds. He thought she'd been dead only a couple of hours but said they'd have to wait for the autopsy to determine cause and manner of death. They took her to the ME's office in the white van."

"Took her down the service elevator?"

"Yes."

"Good."

Sam was glad Aggie had gone and didn't linger to see Monica. Aggie had fears of her own. After being seduced at a young age and impregnated by a jerk who had no real interest in her or a baby, Aggie had avoided men for a long time. The fiasco happened right under Sam's nose when Aggie shared the same Chicago apartment building with him and his wife, Katy. He'd been too preoccupied going to law school to notice Aggie's distress. He didn't notice a lot of things, like how he was better suited for police work than law, so he could catch criminals and not have to defend the guilty ones later.

Aggie was skittish about intimacy. He'd take things slow. Actually, that was the way he wanted it. This was for keeps.

After losing his wife and daughter in the accident, he had his own issues. He was frozen, unable to thaw enough to risk loving again. He'd mostly gotten over his reticence, but there were still moments.

With her unfailing humor and headstrong curiosity, Aggie intrigued him. She'd find a wrong to be righted and flip her swingy hair toward the target like a puppy on point. Who could resist that?

He stood at the door to the suite and pictured the frail girl who had laid there, her head on a bright pillow, cuddling another one, with her dress smoothed down. It was as though the killer did what he came to do, positioned her in serene repose and left. Sick.

He hadn't seen any evidence of trauma or rape on the girl. He was glad for that, especially since Aggie insisted on seeing her. She looked young, angelic and vulnerable.

He wondered how Aggie viewed Monica. Maybe she reminded Aggie of herself as a young girl, seduced and abandoned. Aggie never called it rape, but from her pained expression when she told him about it, he surmised it might have been forceful, at least rough.

Aggie might be in shock. No wonder she didn't respond to his option of their staying in the hotel's utilitarian bedrooms. He wanted her to know he still wanted them to be together, but it didn't seem to register. He guessed his timing was terrible. Yet she seemed to resent his suggestion that she return home and stay away from this tragedy.

It didn't help that Officer Valerie Garret twitched around looking sexy and batting her eyelashes. He was immune to Valerie, but Aggie's antennas shot up.

Since Aggie appreciated and understood his work, he'd rely

on that. Even with Rick as lead detective, he couldn't get away from this crime. The case landed in his lap. He wasn't sure he wanted to get completely away from the murder of a girl related to Aggie's friend Grace. He'd have to be very professional, but he'd let Aggie assist if she was safe. His greatest fear was she'd delve into evil she couldn't handle and he'd lose her. He'd reassure her that this latest debacle in their relationship would pass.

He wanted to go through the scene again and conceptualize for himself what happened. He went into the bathroom and looked around. Officers had marked an indention on the bathroom rug where the girl could have fallen, but from what? There was no evidence she hit her head. Had she fainted and been dragged to the sofa? Above the spot where she fell, a rectangle marked the surface of the countertop, probably from the vanity tray officers bagged along with the contents.

Smelling a sweet odor, he looked around the toilet area for spray. Nothing. He pulled back the tub/shower drape and saw a bottle of coconut almond body massage oil in the corner. Didn't some poison smell like almonds?

He heard Rick enter the bathroom.

"Sorry, Sam." Rick pulled on a glove and bagged the body oil. "The stuff smelled strong and the vent fan was loud. I turned it off, got distracted by something in the living room and we forgot to bag the oil."

"No problem. The girl could have been poisoned. There's some poison that smells like almonds...can't remember which one. We can have this analyzed." Sam followed him out, eyeballing the killer's covered shoe marks and girl's heel prints leading to the sofa. "By the way, did she have a cell phone?"

"We didn't find one. Per the manager's request to keep the crime quiet, I've got plainclothes officers interviewing guests from the penthouse and one floor down. Haddock let us use the business offices. He described a roundabout route we can take to leave through the back entrance. I'm ready to wrap up. You?"

"Yeah. We should have the guys report this to Chief so he can handle the media."

"Right. Are you going back to HQ?"

"Yeah, to type my supplemental report. I'll make sure he knows what we found."

"Okay. Good."

He followed Rick outside the hotel. He was grateful there were no onlookers or press reporters. He might as well go to Headquarters and see what problems awaited him.

He drove to HQ thinking about Aggie trying to comfort the woman she loved like a mother. Could there be a more painful wrench in his and Aggie's relationship? Once she got over the shock, sadness and hurt, she might be more headstrong than usual tracking this killer. With Aggie, you could never be sure.

He'd try to be patient while he waited for reports from the crime lab. He dreaded attending the autopsy.

Seven

Learning about the Femmes from Sara Giles was a good distraction, but I needed to see Grace. Deciding to leave my bags in hotel storage, I commanded my espadrilles to carry me out the front door of the hotel to wait for my car. Albatross and I twisted our way back to Broadway and drove north toward Hildebrand. The farther I got from downtown, the fewer decorations I saw and the heavier my heart felt.

I remembered our outing a week ago. Grace asked me to go with her and Monica to eat at Casa Rio. The building was a hacienda from the 1700s which sat on the original Spanish land grant. We parked on Commerce Street and walked to river level down steps on the first bridge ever constructed over the river.

Monica moved like a butterfly, lithe, airy and free. We found seats at one of Casa Rio's patio tables overlooking the River Walk. Paper flowers decorated restaurant walls. Watermelon runners ran down the center of tables. We dipped nachos into the best chile con queso I'd ever tasted.

Monica pointed to the chile con queso and hot sauce. "A Maitre d' at a restaurant in Piedras Negras, Mexico threw ingredients together to feed hungry army wives at his restaurant in 1943," she said. "His name was Ignacio 'Nacho' Anaya. Thus"—she held one up—"we have nachos."

We sipped margaritas and listened to Monica recount her favorite Fiesta memories while we ate guacamole salad, cheese enchiladas and beef tacos. We loved talking about upcoming Fiesta events. Grace treated Monica like a daughter.

After lunch, we went inside the restaurant to see the building's original stone fireplace. In an adjoining room, Mariachis played and sang for a happy group. The manager told us tales about an Indian who supposedly haunted upstairs rooms. When an employee turned off an upstairs light after closing, lights in other rooms turned off sporadically.

"Whenever we hear noises upstairs," he said, "a staff member tells me, 'the Indian is making noise.'"

"Why an Indian?" I asked.

"Spanish missionaries came here to convert the Indians to Christianity about the same time this building was built."

"I don't believe in ghosts," I said.

"I don't either," Monica said. "There are too many real problems to expend energy worrying about things you can't see."

We walked from the patio down a few steps to river level and boarded a river barge, one of the fleet of boats Casa Rio owned until the city decreed the boat concession should be open to bids. Yanaguana Cruises submitted the low bid but continued to use Casa Rio's boats. We floated by fragrances of angel's trumpet and confederate jasmine flowering alongside the river. We laughed and pointed out landmarks to each other as the barge wound us down the waterway through sunlight and under the shade of overhanging trees. We floated without cares as though suspended in a dream.

I remembered the photograph of Monica and Michael Peters on Grace's buffet. They looked like newlyweds. Michael was the son of Ray Peters, Grace's beloved husband. Grace was previously widowed, and she and Ray had been married a few short years when Ray died.

The last time I saw Grace, she still talked about Ray and how their thoughts roamed together. They were soul mates. She thought when she died and joined him, they'd be caught up on what happened while they were separated. I supposed she'd drawn closer to Monica to help keep Ray's memory alive. Michael still worked in California.

I was startled to find I had driven through traffic without remembering it. When I pulled up to Grace's curb, an SAPD officer was about to get back in his patrol car. I parked behind him and stepped out.

"Ms. Mundeen? I'm Officer Castillo."

"You told her?"

He nodded.

"How is she?"

"In shock, I think. It was quite a blow. She didn't cry out but blinked tears from her eyes and collapsed into the nearest chair. I told her you were coming. She said to leave the front door unlocked."

"Good. Thank you, Officer."

My legs grew leaden when I walked toward her door. "Grace?" It was strange that Boffo didn't bark.

"Come in, Aggie."

I found her in the sunroom, sitting on a striped Sunbrella chair. She looked up with red-rimmed eyes and shook her head from side to side, asking "Why?" without words.

More white strands than I remembered protruded from her gray hair. Boffo sat with his nose by her feet. When I approached, he lifted his head and growled.

We had a history, Boffo and I. He was a Dauschund-Terrier combination, an Earthdog bred to route varmints from tunnels. Because my feet moved and were unfamiliar objects to him, he thought they were varmints. During our adversarial relationship, he used to attack my shoes. I expended a lot of energy gaining Boffo's friendship. When I bent to hug Grace, he wagged his tail, then resumed his guard position with his cheek pressed against her leg.

In the center of the room, a metal rectangular side table

stood on plastic sheeting covered with multi-colored tiles, a spatula and a stirring spoon. Rubber gloves spotted with dried grout flopped over the sides of a grout bucket used for her latest tiling project. Without Grace's infectious enthusiasm, her collection of tools for tiling tables looked like dead relics.

Her eyes exuded pain. "Why would anyone kill Monica?"

"I don't know, Grace. She was lovely." I'd never forget sunlight streaming on her pretty face where she lay draped over the sofa. "Sam is there with other officers. Do you know of any problems she's had lately?"

Grace looked out into the yard. "Well, there was the divorce. She met Michael when he was on location in California with a film crew. She found it glamorous that he was part of the movie industry. They were inseparable and married right away. But when Ray went out a year later to visit them, he said Monica was frustrated having to follow Michael around to work at various locations. The film company didn't pay him much, and their expenses mounted. Monica felt like a burdensome vagabond. They were married about two years before she told him she wanted a divorce. It broke Michael's heart when she left him to enlist in the Army. She said if she had to travel, she might as well get paid for it."

"She was stationed here at Ft. Sam Houston?"

"Yes. When her service ended, she decided not to re-enlist and stayed in San Antonio. I saw her when she first arrived and could see Ray was fond of her. She and I talked on the phone every couple weeks. After he died, she brought memories of him closer. I always wanted a daughter, and I'd secretly pretend she was mine. We grew close. I know the divorce was painful for her, even though she knew their marriage could never work. Just before we all went out, she'd been sort of down and declined my invitation to come over for supper. I thought eating by the river would be a good outing."

"We had a wonderful time." I balanced Grace's comment about Monica seeming depressed against what Sam said about the possibility of her dying from drugs. I was reluctant to jump in and ask about it, so I probed around the edges. "She was honorably discharged?"

"Oh, yes. She liked the service. Her Commanding Officer recommended her for Officer Candidate School, but I think she was ready to be on her own and stay in one place. She made friends here. She joined some women's group, the Feminists, something like that."

"Could it be the Femmes? The Fabulous Femmes?"

"I think that was it. A few months after her divorce, she perked up and started dating again. She said she was making the rounds and having fun. She wasn't interested in a serious relationship. Then lately, she seemed sad."

"Did she say who she dated?"

"Various people she met. Some military men, I think. She didn't mention anybody specific."

"When was the last time you talked to her?"

"Before we went to lunch? About two weeks, give or take." Her eyes filled.

I went over and hugged her again. "Grace, I'm so sorry about Monica."

"I know. It's so hard to take it in. Are you coming home?"

"I think I'll go back to the hotel for a while. It's the Casa Prima. Do you need anything? Groceries?"

She shook her head.

"You have my cell phone number, right?"

She nodded.

"I can be here in ten minutes."

"Okay."

I headed for her front door before my own eyes filled. Boffo didn't bother to bark.

Eight

I asked the valet to park my car, ignoring his disdainful perusal of Albatross. Maybe he didn't appreciate togetherness. Loyalty. Dedication. I loved Albatross. My Wagoneer might be old, but she'd hauled friends and precious items and had gotten me out of some tough spots. Like the long-winged seabird who shared her name, Albatross spent most of her life in flight. With me inside.

When her parts didn't work, she could be an encumbrance. Like I was to Sam when my dogged determination to solve a crime put me in danger. Or in jail. But those were paltry reasons to sever a long-term relationship.

Squaring my shoulders, I entered Casa Prima. Scanning the lobby, I didn't see any sign of Sam or the Fabulous Femmes. I peered inside the restaurant and recognized the two women the police officers had interviewed in the lobby when I arrived this morning. The slim woman adjusted her Hermès scarf, her hands jingling with charm bracelets. The woman in multi-colored neon stripes had a cherubic face surrounded by curls and a smile that lit up the room. I bet she was a lot of fun. They, and the man sitting with them, looked up when I approached. I smiled.

"I've been admiring your scarf," I told the taller woman.

"Thanks."

The neon-sheathed girl smiled. "We saw you in the lobby earlier."

I turned to her. "Are you part of the Fabulous Femmes? I'm Aggie Mundeen. I've been wondering about your group."

"It's absolutely the best. Would you like to sit down? We'll tell you about it. I'm a Flamboyant, Phyllis Morgan. Just remember F sounds, Flamboyant Phyllis."

Phyllis had a circular face, doll eyes and a pleasing plumpness that made me think of Tollhouse Cookies.

My stomach growled. I'd been subsisting on the Healthi/Happy Meals program for a month trying to lose pounds before my River Walk debut in Fiesta attire. The food reminded me of meals ready to eat, MREs, for soldiers starving out in the field. I was finally getting used to eating them, but my stomach had shrunk. My taste buds, having nearly expired, lay dormant. I doubted that even HHM MREs would be effective for wearing Victoria's Secret garb.

"This is my boyfriend," Phyllis said. "John Abbott." John nodded and rose to pull a chair out for me. I loved Southern manners. He had perfect teeth and light eyes that showed up against his tan. His military crew cut looked good with the body he kept in shape. I caught the waiter's eye and ordered a double-protein shake and salad with extra celery and tomatoes to liven it up.

"I'm Felicia Strong, a Foxy Fixit," the chic woman said. "Foxy Felicia is easy enough to remember, but everyone calls me Foxy."

With perfectly coifed blonde hair, expensively-smooth makeup without a single line and lips the color of iced peaches that ran through her Hermès scarf, she was the epitome of Foxy.

"So you're having your convention here?"

"Yes," said Foxy. "We've been planning for years to get the whole group to San Antonio during Fiesta for our annual convention. And now this tragedy. At our hotel!"

I put my finger to my lips.

"Police asked us to keep silent about what we know so as not to scare other guests."

Foxy nodded and lowered her voice. "I've talked to heads of all the groups. Everybody agrees that after waiting so long to get here, we're staying."

"It really is tragic," I said, speaking more quietly. "Did you know the poor girl? Her name was Monica Peters." If they knew her, they might know something about her. When my salad arrived, I stabbed a tomato.

"Monica danced with us in New Orleans," Phyllis whispered.

"She danced?" I rolled the tomato around my mouth, savoring the flavor. I'd take time to put salt on the next bite.

"Sometimes we put on a show at our conventions, simple dance routines," Phyllis explained, her hands gesturing. "One of our members is a choreographer. We get local costumes and find appropriate music. Even though we're not professionals, we have a lot of fun. In New Orleans, we dressed like royal jesters and danced to the Mardi Gras Mamba. Monica was adorable. Loved to have a good time, like all the Flamboyants."

John nodded, his face full of pleasure as he gazed at Phyllis.

Foxy flipped her hair.

"Monica knew how to turn on the charm, that's for sure. Hank loved it."

"Who's Hank?" I asked, crunching salt-and-pepper-laden celery.

"Just the most gorgeous specimen ever to don a uniform. Hank Gleason."

"You should know," Phyllis said to Foxy. "You dated him too. Those of us who live near San Antonio have all dated men who are or were in the military. Isn't that right, John?"

"You bet, "John said. "I didn't know there was any other kind."

"I saw a lot of Texas and US flags rippling in front of businesses on my way down here," I said.

"They honor our service personnel as well as our state and country," John said, "since Army and Air Force bases are an integral part of San Antonio. I guess you know the history of the Alamo."

"I know it symbolizes Texas' independence."

"It sure does," he said. "The Alamo was a Spanish outpost and mission. Mexican General Santa Anna brought five thousand men to capture it so he could add territory to Mexico. But a hundred and eighty 'Texians,' Mexicans and Anglos, stayed to defend the mission. They knew they were significantly outnumbered and would probably die, but they held out for thirteen days before being defeated. A month later, other 'Texians' defeated Santa Anna's army at the Battle of San Jacinto, secured Texas' independence and entrenched the state's mindset of never giving up. Texas relished her independence and remained a Republic for nine years before joining the United States."

"That explains a lot," I said. I'd eaten half my salad and poured hot sauce on the last tomato.

Foxy, looking bored with John's chatter, sighed and looked out toward the river. Then she leaned forward over the table and flashed her eyes, apparently eager to get back to our earlier conversation. "You know, Phyllis, how some members of your Flamboyant group are...well, you know. Let's just say they get around. Monica was like that. The maid too."

Having met Monica and Sara, I found it hard to believe they were as wild as Foxy implied. Grace said Monica was making the rounds, but why shouldn't she? She wasn't interested in re-marrying. Sara saw two men enter and leave Monica's room, but that didn't prove anything.

"Well, I like the maid," Phyllis said. "Her name, by the way, is Sara Giles. Her work as a maid is fairly recent." She continued quietly. "And I liked Monica too. After we danced in that first show together, I got to know her better. Flamboyants are always friendly and fun. They just enjoy having a good time. What's wrong with that?"

"Not a thing." I was fortified with protein and feeling feisty. That's all I ever wanted, a man I loved who loved me, a job that challenged me and to have some fun. After I stumbled on a dead body the first time and Sam showed up from SAPD Homicide, I realized how invigorating criminal investigation could be. You could track down an evil person and make him pay for the misery he caused. Persistent curiosity landed me into predicaments that didn't always turn out well, of course. Still, you had to follow your hunches. I scraped lettuce from the bowl and slugged the last of the protein drink.

"Maybe Sara *was* a Flamboyant a long time ago," Foxy said, "before her husband dumped her. No more gallivanting around after that. Now she's cleaning other people's rooms." Foxy leaned back, smoothed her hair and admired the three-karat diamond on her right hand.

"By the way," she said, "the Fiesta Commission changed the schedule. They told us at the meeting yesterday that Night in Old San Antonio is only two nights this year, Monday and Tuesday. I have to welcome everybody to La Villita. The Texas Cavaliers will honor the military with their river parade on Wednesday night so military units have time to get ready. We have dance practice on Tuesday, so we'll be ready for our Arneson Theater show at the Wednesday night parade. If we're going to NIOSA, Monday, tomorrow night, is the time to go."

"Who are the Cavaliers?" I asked.

"They're a socially prominent group of city leaders and professional men who raise money for children's charities and elect King Antonio annually to reign over Fiesta. They put on the

Fiesta River Parade every year." Foxy sat straighter. "I've dated several of them." She looked at her watch. "Our Madhatter, Martha Mayberry, ought to be here with Roger pretty soon. He and John are Army brats," she told me. "They've known each other for years. Do you want to stroll the river with us?"

"I might go with my boyfriend later."

"Okay. Maybe we'll see you there. Why don't you come to our dance practice Tuesday night in the ballroom? It's fun to watch. Do you like to dance?"

"I love to dance. Sometimes I'm a little klutzy, but with a good beat, I do pretty well."

"You should come. You might want to join in."

A third woman and her boyfriend arrived, Madhatter Martha Mayberry and Roger Plunkett. Martha was a tall redhead with freckles sprinkled across her nose above a wide smile. A crop of vibrant ten-inch paper sunflowers gorilla-glued on top of her floppy-brimmed hat made her even taller. She gave Roger credit for the creation.

He was tall too, with a military bearing and short dark hair and eyes. Unlike John, he hadn't acquired a Texas tan. He wore a long shirt that hung out over his pants. His chest was covered with Fiesta medals arranged in perfectly straight rows, probably from the military influence.

"You've got quite a collection of medals there," I said.

"Thanks. I try to find new ones every year," Roger said. "I'm always on the hunt for rare medals. It's fun to collect them."

"Who started the tradition?"

"They say the Cavaliers' King Antonio handed out commemorative coins at Fiesta events in 1946. Then in 1971, King Antonio and his commander sat in the Menger Hotel lobby with hammers and nails and punched holes in two hundred fifty King's coins. They attached red, white and blue lapel ribbons and created the first Fiesta medals. Now organizations sell medals to raise funds, and businesses use them to advertise. Military units give theirs away."

"*Love* your sunflower hat," Phyllis told Martha. "John made me a hat of solar panels to wear at NIOSA to advertise his business. He's been working on it for weeks. I haven't seen it yet, but he says it will make me look taller."

The outfits people conjured up for Fiesta fascinated me. As the group waved goodbye, I noticed water bottles sticking from the men's back pockets. Good idea. San Antonio was getting hot. Instead of wearing espadrilles, Foxy had on strappy sandals with three-inch heels. They were gorgeous but would kill most people navigating flagstones on the River Walk.

I didn't know where Sam was or whether he'd want to stroll the river. I hadn't even decided whether to stay.

Nine

A man entered the restaurant and looked around. He drew my attention because he had black flashing eyes, well-groomed hair and wore a business suit with four Fiesta medals flanking the brass name tag on his coat pocket. His gaze settled on me.

"Ms. Agatha Mundeen?"

I'd never been called "Ms." so often. It was beginning to annoy me. But I was glad this man was looking for me. I sat straighter. "Yes?"

He walked over, extended his hand, took mine in a warm, firm grasp and produced a winsome smile. "I'm Harry Haddock, Hotel Manager. Detective Vanderhoven said you might like to see some rooms?"

"Yes, I would. Thank you."

When I stood, he touched my elbow lightly and steered me out of the restaurant. Waitresses smiled at him as we passed. We waited for the next elevator, and he pushed the button to the third floor.

"As I told the detective, we have a couple of rooms that are primarily utilitarian. When the hotel was built, they were an afterthought, a place for employees or maintenance people who became ill or who, for some reason, had to stay here overnight. They're quite clean and functional, but they're not luxurious like the guest rooms, certainly not like the suites."

We were alone on the elevator, but he lowered his voice. "I

understand you were booked in the penthouse suite, the room where the poor girl was killed." He blanched.

River Walk hotels were prime real estate. After fifty years or so, a hotel might entice guests with stories of historical ghosts floating around. But nobody wanted newly-minted ghosts tromping through hotels during Fiesta Week. I understood why he was upset she was dead, but why did he assume she was killed?

We got off at three and turned left down the hallway. He stopped at an unmarked room and opened the room with a standard key. We entered a nine-by-nine cubicle with a tiny window and a bathroom with a shower off to the side. The bed, about thirty inches wide with a metal arc for a headboard, reminded me of hospital beds lined up down long rooms in old movies. I wondered if Sam could even sleep in the narrow bed without falling off. It definitely wouldn't hold two people. There was no other furniture, only a tiny closet.

"Like I said, the rooms are strictly utilitarian. There's another one on five." He closed the door, and we walked back toward the elevator. I glanced around the ceiling for video cameras, spotted one across from the elevator and decided to get his reaction. "I see you have video cameras."

"All hotels have them."

The fifth-floor room was somewhat larger, perhaps nine by twelve, with a small desk, chair and lamp against one wall. The bed looked even narrower.

"If you use the internet, this room has a receptacle where you can plug in your computer."

"I do get occasional email." I decided not to tell him I wrote a column. He might think I was an investigative reporter. "Has anyone vacated guest rooms because of the crime?"

"Not yet. We're keeping the tragedy quiet, of course."

The Femmes knew. Everybody in the penthouse knew. By

now, everybody on staff probably knew, although they wore Chamber of Commerce smiles like nothing had happened.

"People book rooms way ahead for Fiesta Week," he said. "So they're reluctant to give them up. If something opens up, you and the detective will be the first to know."

I took a guess. "Speaking of Detective Vanderhoven, he thought you knew Monica Peters?"

"I met her several times. She rented a suite every year for a week during Fiesta and was a quiet, charming guest. This time she came Thursday planning to stay ten days. But she changed her mind and decided to leave Sunday. That's how Detective Vanderhoven was able to rent the suite."

"Because she shortened her stay?"

He shrugged. "I guess she made other plans."

They undoubtedly didn't include dying. What made Monica decide to leave early? I wondered how well he knew her.

"Did Monica mention she'd been in the Army?"

"She told me."

I found it somewhat odd she told the manager since she only stayed at the hotel during Fiesta Week. Maybe he knew her better than he indicated. "She probably dated military personnel," I probed.

"I saw her with a uniformed man in the restaurant. We see a lot of service people in the hotel. After all, it's Military City."

"Was he one of your regular guests too?"

"No, but I've seen him dating various women during Fiesta Week." His frown indicated he thought I was getting nosy.

I wondered if he was talking about Hank Gleason, the handsome officer the Femmes discussed. Gleason apparently had an affinity for a variety of women.

"It's hard to imagine why anyone would kill that young woman."

He nodded.

As we walked back to the elevator, I noticed a door marked "Employees Only" and couldn't resist asking about it.

"It's a storage closet for cleaning supplies the maids use."

Was there a storage closet in the penthouse? Did it house bulbs and backup ceiling fixtures like the ones Sara described? If Monica was killed in the bathroom, maybe I needed to see what was in there.

I'd never get into the crime scene bathroom. Either SAPD officers were still there or the door to the suite would be locked. Sam probably stationed an officer inside the lounge to watch whether anyone unauthorized tried to enter.

I was dying to ask Harry more questions about Monica to probe how well he knew her and find out who else he saw her with, but I didn't want to make him suspicious.

"Thank you so much for the tour, Mr. Haddock. I'll keep those rooms in mind in case no regular vacancies occur."

"I'll leave keys to the rooms at registration with your and Detective Vanderhoven's names on them. Employees have to clear it with me before using them."

"On second thought, why don't you give me the key to the room on five. I can use my laptop there."

He handed me the key. I followed him to the check-in desk to claim my bag from storage, dragged it into the elevator and rolled it down the hall on the fifth floor to install it in my cubbyhole.

Ten

Sam

Sam parked in the lot on W. Nueva near Headquarters. He wasn't anxious to go in. He'd barely settled into relief-day mindset and wasn't ready to go back to work. He dragged himself into the first-floor Homicide Unit at four thirty.

Criminal Investigations Division (CID) included the Homicide Unit, Sex Crimes and smaller units of White Collar Crimes and Forgery. Sam's unit wasn't only Homicide investigations. It was all crimes against persons. "Agg" detectives handled Aggravated Assaults, violent felony offenses where complainants did not die. Other detectives handled misdemeanors, and Traffic Investigation Division (TID) investigated fatality accidents and traffic related offences. In the perceived pecking order, murder guys thought they were at the top, Aggs weren't all that impressed with murder guys, and the others thought both were overrated. Sam had been there long enough to know perception didn't always equal reality.

By the time he arrived, Homicide Unit's forty to fifty detectives had been working since eight a.m., were tired of their four-by-six-foot office cubicles and waited for six p.m. when they could go home. Some worked on unfinished business. Others waited for a witness to come in to give a statement, hoping to get overtime.

Cubicles were decorated with family photos, newspaper

articles derisive of the department's administration or some particular investigation. Cartoons and nicknames made fun of co-workers. Detectives needed distractions to perk up the eggshell walls painted with gray trim, not to mention working four dangerous or depressing ten-hour days followed by three RDs off, their relief days. Sam had accrued enough time for an extra relief day.

Two units across the hall made up Sex Crimes and Night Detectives. A lot of detectives in Sam's unit started out grumpy in the morning when they got work left over from Night Detectives, who worked from seven p.m. until three a.m. By this time of day, there were pranks, cursing and blaming Division Chiefs and the Police Chief on the second floor if detectives thought higher-ups were trying to direct their homicide investigations.

With all the recent drive-by shootings, some detectives got three or four cases a month. One of the Police Chief's goals was to stop having the city known as the "drive-by capital." Daytime detectives frequently thought Night Detectives should get answers to more questions from defendants before handing cases over to them.

Pranks and cursing were currently in full swing, especially among the homicide detectives. He wasn't surprised to catch flak just walking to his desk.

"Hey, Romeo, I thought you had a special thing coming up. You tired already?"

"Hear you were so busy you had to call Montaya in to help. That right?"

Sam mumbled a few choice words and went to his cubicle. He was glad they didn't know Aggie's name. They'd have a field day with it.

He was glad his cubicle was near the center of the room. After a season of sewer problems plaguing the building, detectives whose cubicles backed up to the restroom wall were burning scented candles on their desks.

Except for a few inconsequential memos, his desk was clear. He ignored the fracas going on around him and thought about the crime scene. He kept thinking about shoe marks left on the carpet. It was the only visual clue they had to the killer. Where did he get shoe coverings?

Nix Hospital was near the hotel. He thought they should go there and see what they could learn about the booties doctors and nurses wore over their shoes. He'd mention it to Rick.

He looked around for his sergeant.

"You found a body in a River Walk hotel?" the sergeant asked.

"Yes, sir. She was apparently in good health, age twenty-nine, here to enjoy Fiesta. Detective Montaya and I are handling it as a suspicious death until the autopsy results tell us differently. There were no trauma marks or bleeding and nothing out of place. Then we saw two sets of footprints on the carpet, one pair that looked like covered shoes walking backward toward the sofa where we found the body with her heel prints dragging along after them. The body looked like somebody positioned it."

"No contact with the media?"

"No, sir. The hotel manager was worried about publicity. EMS and the MEs used the back entrance of the hotel."

The sergeant would find the Homicide Lieutenant who would pass it to the CID Captain who would inform the Chief. Sam knew Chief Brigham would still be there. He was always last to leave.

The sergeant came back to fill him in. "Seems the Public Information Officer got a call from a reporter. Chief told him it was an unfortunate death, probably a personal quarrel, nothing to alarm Fiesta goers."

"Got it."

Sam finished typing his Supplement Report. There wasn't much more he could do except wait. He'd go back to the hotel and dress to go on the river. He hoped he could turn around in the ridiculously small shower. The bed would barely fit a large child. Two adults? He couldn't picture it.

Eleven

I heaved my suitcase on the bed, zipped it open and considered what I'd packed: bright casual clothes, flip-flops, tennis shoes, sandals, sunscreen, a sun hat and wedged shoes for sundresses, plus the swim suit I bought after trying on fifty others with a wrap that tied over the suit and covered me from waist to ankle. I brought enough makeup, shampoo and hair products to stock a pharmacy. With my computer added, my suitcase was pretty heavy.

I spent too much for spray liquid tan, but tan fat looked better than white fat. When I went to Victoria's Secret and saw my image in the mirror, I doubled over with laughter. Ultimately, I made a purchase, but I also packed lounging pajamas, normal pajamas, and my Garfield sleep shirt in case my romantic reluctance turned to panic. What if Sam laughed uproariously when he saw me in Victoria's garb?

Ever since I cruised past thirty-five, I'd dreaded middle-age. Pushing forty, I felt inadequate, inexpert and growing older by the minute.

I hung clothes in the closet and shoved my luggage on the floor underneath. Locating a socket behind the small desk, I plugged in my computer and decided to perk myself up by answering Dear Aggie readers. The newspaper would forward email letters they received addressed to Dear Aggie. Before leaving for my rendezvous with Sam, I asked Grace to check my snail mail to Dear Aggie and email me the contents. Even besieged with grief for Monica, I knew Grace wouldn't forget.

Writing "Stay Young with Aggie" was the perfect job for me. With middle-age approaching like a runaway train, I was intrigued by exercise, products and miracles that promised to prevent decrepitude. I loved sharing what I leaned.

I clicked on an email from Grace. Sure enough, Barbara in Baltimore wrote to Dear Aggie.

Dear Aggie,

I've been in love with Theo for over a year. He comments about "overly-healthy" women, so I've been trying to lose weight. I bought a three-month membership at a health club and workout clothes with spandex liners. The pants were so tight I had to take pills to ease the pain. They made me oblivious to pain and everything else. Not good. I started a walking regimen and low-carb diet, which is working, but slowly. Theo wants us to take a beach vacation in two months, which means I'll have to wear a swim suit. Any advice?

Bulging in Baltimore,
Barbara

Dear Barbara,

I've tried every weight reduction plan on the planet. I have felt your pain. After exercising, I've had to soak in a hot tub gulping Advil and follow the bath with a rejuvenating nap in order to resume functioning. You and Theo may have made wookie in the dark, but at the beach, he will see more of you in your glory. Here's my advice about swim suits: the tensile strength of Lycra has improved. Get a big enough swimsuit or you will look like a stuffed sausage. You don't want your boobs flattened and spread across your chest like a speed bump. Make sure the suit has an underwire bra or definable cups unless you want your chest to look like rolled pie dough. After you fight your way into the suit, make sure no part of you oozes out from the Lycra. If something escapes, stuff it back in. Make sure you can breathe. Don't go for a matronly swim suit with a skirt. Avoid any suit with a floral pattern. Flowered Hippo is not a good look anywhere except at Disney. Go for a one-piece style in black or navy. Whatever our body type, we all look slimmer in black and navy. Use spray tan beforehand so your legs won't look like cottage cheese. Play it safe. Spring for a flattering cover up to match the suit that ties around your waist and ends at your ankles. Make sure your hair is full and shiny, have your nails and toes perfectly groomed, wear sunscreen, glossy lipstick, sexy sunglasses and smile a lot. The idea is to accentuate your best features. Those are what he sees because he cares about you.

Been there,
Aggie

I wrenched on my swim suit, recalling the agony of trying on the other fifty contenders. Valerie Garrett undoubtedly looked a lot better in swimsuits and lingerie than I ever would. It was stupid to be jealous of Valerie. She was just somebody Sam worked with. A lot.

Maybe Victoria's Secret would let me return the skimpy lingerie. It wasn't even comfortable. I couldn't try it on without laughing. Talk about buyer's remorse.

To pigment my pasty skin, I'd slathered bronze-tinted self-tanning lotion on my legs for days. Over my black swimsuit, I wrapped a waist-to-ankle cover up. Black around my waist and hips, it changed to navy lower down, then to turquoise and an eye-catching peacock blue when it hit my ankles. Sexy golden sandals set off my Neon Fuchsia toenail polish. Certain parts must be emphasized over others.

After skillfully arranging the cover up, I greased exposed body areas with moisturizing sunscreen, washed my hands, grabbed my hat and made my way to the elevator.

In the lobby, revelers in Fiesta attire milled about, laughing as they filed in and out from the River Walk. The fragrance of blooming honeysuckle wafted through the lobby as I made my way to the pool.

People were beginning to show up poolside. A chaise lounge next to an umbrella-shaded table looked perfect. A beautiful anaqua tree was planted not far behind it. Hampered by the cover up, I quick-stepped toward the chaise to nab it before anyone could get there and placed my hat on the table so it was obvious I was claiming it. I leaned back in the chaise, kicked off my sandals, exposed my newly tanned legs up to the fleshy part and closed my eyes, enjoying the breeze and sunshine.

The sun hiding behind a cloud made me blink my eyes open in time to see Sara Giles enter the pool area.

Twelve

Sara had gotten rid of her uniform and changed to Capri pants and a gauzy shirt. Foxy passed behind her in the hotel and turned up her nose. I motioned Sara over.

"Come sit down." I grabbed the nearest chair and scraped it over the concrete.

"Thanks. I'm through for the day. I'm so glad to get out of the hotel. I get tired of smelling nothing but air conditioning."

"I'm glad we're getting to visit. Let's get nachos and something to drink. Lemonade? Wine?"

"White wine, I think. It's been a long day."

"And a sad one."

She nodded. I motioned to the waiter on our side of the pool and gave our order. "I've been wondering about different groups in the Femmes. Can you tell me more about them?"

"Sure. Madhatters like to express themselves through their hats for fun. It's a great icebreaker."

I wouldn't dare wear a hat to express my moods. A Sherlock Holmes hat for sleuthing? An egghead hat for taking classes? A Valentine hat around Sam? Too revealing.

"You've met Martha Mayberry?" she asked.

"She seems delightful. Always smiling." I grinned. "When I met her, she was wearing a garden of huge paper sunflowers Roger glued on her hat."

"That's Madhatter Martha. She can have fun, look silly and

laugh at herself. She's just a happy person. Roger adores her."

I wanted to be like that. Carefree. Happy. Not prone to worry. But when someone was wronged, I grew doggedly intense.

"Phyllis said John Abbott made some kind of hat with panels to wear on her head," I said. "She'll be so busy balancing panels, I don't think she'll have much fun at NIOSA. She's a Flamboyant, right?"

"Yes. So was I." The waiter brought us wine and water. We sat and sipped. My wine didn't taste good. It was hard to get in a party mood.

She looked out over people playing in the pool. "It seems like eons ago," she mused, "when I was a Flamboyant having fun. Monica Peters was a Flamboyant too. That's how I met her. After we spent time together dancing in the show at Mardi Gras, I'd see her here when she'd stay downtown for Fiesta. We attended some Fiesta events together. I can't believe she's gone."

"Didn't Phyllis Morgan dance with you too? She's also a Flamboyant, right?"

"Yes."

"Tell me about the Flamboyants and about Monica."

"Well, we like to wear outrageous clothes to draw attention. We're party girls who enjoy a good time. Fundamentally, I guess we're people pleasers. We do things to attract attention and make people like us. Like Phyllis wearing that ridiculous hat to please John." She took another sip. "I used to be like that. I concentrated so much on pleasing my husband I became a doormat. People get bored with doormats. At least he did."

Sara and I had that in common. At eighteen, I was undeniably a doormat. Why else had I succumbed to Lascivious Lester? At least I'd learned to stand up for myself. The problem was, sometimes I overdid it to the point where I didn't listen to anybody. Sam would agree.

"I understand how that is," I said. "I was definitely a doormat." I felt very comfortable with Sara and decided to confide in her. "Monica Peters was step-daughter-in-law to my dear friend Grace. She loved Monica like a daughter. Detective Sam Vanderhoven and I are very close, and we desperately want to find Monica's killer. I know she was recovering from a divorce. Do you think she was like us, a doormat?" Sara's glass was empty. I motioned to the waiter for refills.

"I think she had been. She told me she fell madly in love with her former husband to the point she agreed to anything. She followed him all over California until he felt like he was being pursued by a dark shadow. She felt like a tagalong, unhappy and alone while he worked. Monica liked to be with people, talk with them, get to know them. She felt like an unwanted stalker."

I remembered Monica at Casa Rio, talking to the waiter, the water boy and the manager. I could tell she wouldn't mind dropping in at the private party and joining them to hear the Mariachis.

"Monica finally decided to end their marriage and enlist in the service." She took a sip. "During her time in the Army, I think she grew up and became her own person, equal to anyone she dated."

"She didn't re-enlist, right?"

"Right. She did well while she was there. I think she was just finally ready to be on her own."

"She continued to date Army men?"

"Yes. Non-commissioned officers at first, then officers. As an enlistee, she'd had quite enough of being the low girl on the totem pole. She was promoted as quickly as anyone, but when she was discharged, she was no longer interested in dating NCOs. Only officers."

"Anyone in particular?"

"Not that I know of. The minute a man became dictatorial or possessive, which can be characteristic of high-ranking officers, she was gone."

After meeting Monica, I could imagine her not wanting to be controlled or tied to any one person. "I understand she recently dated an officer. Do you know who he was?"

"I don't know. But I can tell you if he started telling her what to do, he didn't last long."

Had Hank or some other man gotten angry, really angry, when Monica didn't conform to his wishes? Angry enough to kill her?

"What about the Foxy Fixits?"

She chuckled. "The name says it all. They like to run things and are proud of it. Our Fabulous Femmes president, Felicia Strong, came from San Antonio's Foxy Fixits. Foxy's been president of just about every club in this town. After her divorce, she increased her involvement. I don't see how anyone could be interested in that many organizations or charities. I think she just likes to run the show. Well, to each her own."

Foxy did seem the type to run things. I wondered if the donor of her three-karat diamond decided she could keep it as a small price to pay for liberation.

"I've wanted to ask you something," I said, "but maybe you're not supposed to discuss it. I see guests need a room key to make the elevator go up, open the door to their rooms and enter the penthouse. How could somebody without a key get into Monica's suite without forcing entry?"

"I know you're the detective's friend and were Monica's friend, so I don't mind discussing it. Have you ever lost your room key?"

"Sure. I'm always embarrassed when I have to ask somebody at the front desk for another one."

"It's pretty common for guests to lose a key. Sometimes

guests give a key to somebody. I'm afraid that's fairly common too."

I nodded.

"Management and staff have pass keys to everything," she said. "I think hotels need a system like cruise ships have where guests and staff slide keys into a verification slot before re-entering the hotel, activating the elevator or entering their room. Information on the key shows up on a screen that has to match their room registration, photo or employee ID."

Sara would make a good manager. She was perceptive and smart. Her capabilities ran way above cleaning hotel rooms. They should put her in charge of security. Her husband must have been a dumb clod to leave this woman.

"Penthouse room keys also open the door to the lounge, correct?"

"Yes."

"Are penthouse suites all decorated the same? You told me about skylights that look like recessed lights. Were skylights installed other places in the hotel?" I didn't know why I was asking. I just kept picturing light diffusing on Monica's face.

"There are skylights over the entrance to the river and in the garden breakfast room at the side of the hotel." She paused. "It probably doesn't mean anything, but Foxy's husband flirted with Monica at one of our conventions. The next I heard, he filed for divorce. I doubt there's any connection to Monica's death. Flirtations happen. But the reason Foxy puts down the Flamboyants is because her husband found Monica attractive. As a result, some of the Foxy Fixits don't like any of the Flamboyants. I'm glad Phyllis and Foxy remained friends."

Sara had a generous heart. I wonder if she knew how Foxy degraded her.

"Both Foxy and Phyllis get along with Martha Mayberry," she said. "But the Madhatters and Flamboyants have had their differences too. Lots of Madhatters perform in the dance group, so they're opinionated about costumes and music and vocal about what they want. But Cindy, a Flamboyant, is the choreographer and directs the group. She insists on selecting the final choices. There's bad blood there."

"Hmm. I guess there are always problems in a group."

"Yes, and the Fabulous Femmes are all independent women with strong personalities."

"Independence has its own set of problems," I said.

"Don't I know it." She sipped her wine. Mine tasted sour.

Since everybody seemed to know Hank Gleason, I wondered if Sara dated him too. "Did you happen to date Hank Gleason?"

"I met him. But, no. He wouldn't be interested in dating a maid." She took a deep breath, let it out and set down her glass. "This has been a real treat, Aggie, but I better get home. I have to work tomorrow."

"Whenever you take a break, look for me at the pool."

"Okay. Thanks for the wine and nachos," she said. "And the friendship." She produced a sad smile and left.

From behind my trendy Ray Bans, I watched kids cavort in the pool, thinking about Monica and friction between people.

I motioned to the waiter and ordered dip, celery and lemonade with artificial sweetener to fortify myself before our walk on the river. Children frolicking in the pool made a lot of noise, but I thought I could hear over them. I dialed Grace on my cell phone to see how she was.

"I'm okay, I guess. I'm making myself tile that table. It makes me concentrate on that for a while. I tried playing beautiful music but it makes me cry. Then Boffo starts howling."

"Grace, I'm so sorry."

"Have you learned any more about how Monica died?"

I tried to think of something to make her feel better. "There were no signs of struggle, so she wasn't hurt by anyone beating her up. It might've been someone she knew and she let them in." As soon as the words left my lips, I knew they were wrong.

"I see. Dear God."

"I'm so sorry, Grace. Can you remember her saying anything about who she dated? A name? Rank?"

She paused. "No. She primarily dated Army officers. Sergeant? Colonel? Major? I don't know much about rank. She said she liked capable men, even though they could be bossy."

"Well, that's something to go on. Keep working on that table, okay?"

"By the way, I emailed you a letter to Dear Aggie."

"I got it. Thank you."

"There's something else, Aggie. I couldn't bring myself to tell you about it when I'd just learned Monica died. The last time I talked to her, before we went to Casa Rio, she said she was afraid she might be getting in too deep. She knew she didn't want to get married, but she was falling for somebody. That's why she was down. I thought going out and talking about Fiesta Week coming up might help."

"You don't know who the man was?"

"She didn't say. After we came back from lunch on the river, she told me she was two weeks late on her period."

I felt like I'd been punched in the stomach. I sucked in a breath and let it out slowly before I could speak. "I see. We'll find out who did this, Grace."

Thirteen

I drew closer under the umbrella to shield myself from the sun and process what Grace said about Monica. Poor Monica. Poor Grace. It seemed some people were plagued by bad fortune no matter how hard they tried.

I was staring dully out over the pool when I looked up and saw Sam. He'd changed into a loud patterned shirt to look more like a tourist and slicked down his hair with something shiny. The unruly patch in front still shot up. With his hair plastered, he looked weighted with fatigue. His voice was still authoritative. Cop-like. "I thought you might have gone home."

Was he disappointed? With him wearing sunglasses, I couldn't see the doggy-brown eyes I loved. I felt like reaching up to hug his neck. We both needed comforting.

"The desk clerk said you might be here." His tone was mater-of-fact. Impersonal.

I understood where he needed to place his priorities. He had a murder to solve. Since crime eclipsed our rendezvous, I just wished he could consider me a partner in the investigation. I might as well go home, let him handle it and try to comfort Grace. First, I should divulge what I learned.

"I went to see Grace. She's in shock."

"What did she say about Monica?"

"She was married to Michael Peters, the son of Grace's beloved husband, Ray, for about two years. She announced she wanted a divorce and joined the Army. Her last assignment was in San Antonio, and she stayed here after her discharge. Grace grew close to her, thought of her as family and they kept in touch. Monica received an honorable discharge, which I assume meant she had no history of drug use. I didn't have the heart to ask specifically about that. Monica enjoyed dating military men. As far as Grace knew, she didn't have a special boyfriend. But she recently told Grace she was falling for someone, which she didn't want to do. After we came home from lunch last week, Monica told Grace she was two weeks late on her period."

"Grace didn't know who the man was?"

"No."

He leaned forward. He sensed I hadn't told him everything. I needed to practice my poker face.

"What?"

"I just visited with the maid, Sara Giles." I lowered my voice almost to a whisper. "She told the officers that the day before she found Monica she saw two men enter and leave Monica's room."

Sam pulled his chair closer so nobody could hear us. "Yes, the patrol officer told me, but Sara couldn't give much of a description. We're checking video cams from the penthouse but haven't seen anybody enter Monica's room. The camera was focused on the area in front of the elevators. But there were gaps. Somebody could have temporarily disabled it."

"The men could have been Monica's friends, buddies, whoever." Why did I feel compelled to protect Monica's reputation when I barely knew her? I supposed it was because I loved Grace, liked Monica and didn't enjoy hearing Foxy denigrate her. How much did Monica have to do with Foxy's divorce? Probably nothing, but Foxy thought she did. Maybe Foxy married the man for his money and the divorce cost her a bundle.

"We're trying to find somebody who saw the men. We're also checking the address Monica gave the hotel to see if it's current. Somebody near her home might know who she dated."

"Mr. Haddock told me Monica rented a suite every year during Fiesta Week and was a lovely guest," I said. "This time she came Thursday and was scheduled to stay ten days."

"He told me. Did he say why she shortened her stay?"

I shook my head.

He looked at me over his glasses. The hair that escaped the pomade flopped on his forehead. "You've been busy, haven't you?"

I nodded. I tried to understand why he didn't appreciate my eagerness to help, even though I had good ideas and noticed details. I was more tuned to people's psychology than he was. Except for his ability to read me. At least he accepted the fact that I'd made a few inquiries. I simply wanted justice, like he did. I guess it was my headstrong curiosity that got him. He worried about my being hurt. Or killed.

He leaned back in the chair Sara vacated. "Haddock showed you the utility bedrooms?"

"Not much to look at, are they?"

"No."

I tried to be positive. "The room on three isn't too bad. The bed looks a little wider." I paused. "Why don't we just get a room in another hotel?"

"There are no more rooms available anywhere near the River Walk during Fiesta Week. At any price. I called them all. I only got the room here because Monica said she was checking out early."

His voice rose. I put a finger to my lips. He struggled to lower his voice.

"There are a jillion people attending conventions: Southern States Communications, the National Council of English

Teachers, American Language and Hearing Association..." He reeled off a dozen groups. "I was only wait-listed here until the assistant manager left me a message to confirm. I've called more hotels since we found Monica. I need to be in this hotel or close by until we get this thing solved. Most killers return to the scene of the crime. The lower our profile, the more apt he is to return. Somebody needs to be here. I can do surveillance here in plainclothes while Montaya handles the investigation." He sighed and leaned forward.

"As much as I'd like to be with you, Aggie, I think you'll be safer at home. We can have our rendezvous after this is over."

Already inside the hotel, he was first detective on scene. I could see why his staying here offered the best chance to solve the murder and keep guests safe. At least he found us alternative sleeping quarters, unappealing though they were. Separate pigeonhole rooms also served to keep me at arm's length so I wouldn't impede his investigation.

With Sam, I vacillated between understanding and paranoia. It was most likely a self-esteem issue. I blamed Lascivious Lester for that.

My options were to go home, die of curiosity and let him solve the case without me. Or stick around to see what happened and bunk on a Lilliputian cot.

"I got the key to the cubbyhole on the fifth floor," I said, "so I could change into my swim suit and enjoy the pool."

"Okay. I'll use the one on three. At least I can take a shower."

"What else have you learned?" I asked.

He pulled his chair closer and talked softer. "Well, since the killer covered his shoes to distort markings on his shoe sole, Rick went to Nix Hospital to learn about booties doctors and nurses wear to cover their shoes before they enter the OR. He'll verify whereabouts of orderlies and cleaning staff around the time she was killed. But since we don't have a shred of the actual shoe covers, we can't identify their origin or test the inside for sole markings. No pharmacies reported drug theft, and we haven't found evidence of drugs in the suite. The lab might come up with something. There were no prints in the suite except for Monica's and a staff member who took food up her first night here. The hotel telephone log verified she placed the order, and we confirmed the server's whereabouts Saturday and Sunday. The lock hadn't been jimmied, so either somebody had a key to her room or she let them in.

"From his initial look, the ME thinks from the absence of markings on her body, she was poisoned with a liquid or gas. He can't determine what it was or where it came from until they do the autopsy and toxicology screen. The Houston crime lab recently made the newspapers for a mistake, and our lab was just accredited. Scientists are being real careful so it takes a while to get results. Did you learn anything else from Grace?"

"Grace and Sara both said Monica dated Army officers. Officers, not NCOs. If an officer became dictatorial, she lost interested and ditched him. She dated an officer named Hank Gleason who shows up every year and dates available women during Fiesta. Foxy dated him too."

"I'll find out about him. I've seen you talking with the convention ladies. Did they know Monica?"

"Yes. She was a member of the Femmes and a sub-group, the Flamboyants. Phyllis and Martha liked her, but she flirted with Foxy's husband, who is now her ex-husband."

"Maybe there was more than flirting. We'll check into it."

"Foxy gets her kicks from running organizations. I doubt she's a killer. If she lost money in the divorce, she might blame Monica."

"A lawyer I know might be able to obtain their divorce records."

"Sara said there's animosity between sub-groups of the Femmes. Because of Monica, Foxy turned her Fixit friends against the Flamboyants. The Madhatters and Flamboyants got crosswise over costumes and music they use for performances at conventions. It sounds like petty disagreements between groups, not serious vendettas."

"Did you learn who else dated Monica?"

"Phyllis and Martha's boyfriends probably knew Monica, but I don't think they dated her. Roger Plunkett seems crazy about Madhatter Martha Mayberry. You've probably seen him around. His chest is covered with Fiesta medals. He and Phyllis' boyfriend, John Abbott, made their girlfriends crazy hats to wear at NIOSA. Goofy, Fiesta fun. Nothing to point to Monica's killer."

"It's possible the hotel manager dated Monica and didn't appreciate her checking out early. I'll press him about it."

"I doubt he'd commit murder in his own hotel. Talk about hurting business."

"Unless it was a crime of passion." He leaned closer and gave me a penetrating look. "Will you think about what I said?"

"About going home? I haven't decided. I've always wanted to stay in a downtown hotel during Fiesta. I can't wait to stroll the river."

He checked his watch. "All right. I need to check some things. I'll meet you at the river entrance around eight."

Fourteen

I returned to my room and showered in the Lilliputian space, musing about the ME's opinion that Monica was poisoned with a liquid or gas. If she was killed in the bathroom, what did the killer use? If police found no trace of a foreign substance, did he use something common to a bathroom? Officers undoubtedly bagged toiletries and makeup for analysis. I closed my eyes to picture a bathroom and let my eyes roam around. If the counter was clear of soaps and toiletries, the only place left would be underneath the sink. Cleaning products.

Combinations of certain products produced lethal liquids or gas. Police probably checked the cabinets, but what if the killer brought in standard cleaning products, created a lethal combination, killed Monica and took the products with him when he left. Even if trace evidence found residue, traces from standard bathroom cleaners wouldn't cause suspicion.

I powered up my computer. This was a good time to research cleaning products. Maybe later I'd find the opportunity to check stock in the employees' storage closet.

I learned drain cleaners should never be mixed, nor one kind used right after another. Most of them contained lye, hydrochloric acid or trichloroethane. The first two would acid-burn your insides on contact. The last one would depress your nervous system and damage your liver and kidneys. Surely Monica's face or lips would show signs of ingesting those poisons.

Case histories indicated when people routinely used products that weren't harmful, they mixed them without thinking. One man, in his effort to unclog a second-floor toilet, used household bleach, then household ammonia, then drain cleaner. The combination released toxic gases, including chlorine and possibly phosgene gas. He was overcome by the fumes and died.

Some toilet bowl cleaners were acid-based—hydrochloric acids. Others contained the dangerous chemical sodium bisulfate. Poison centers reported people would use a toilet bowl cleaner first. If not satisfied with the results, they would add bleach. The combination produced chlorine gas, sometimes more powerful than gases used in World War I.

What if a maid cleaned Monica's toilet with a standard cleaner? Not pleased with the outcome, she added bleach to the bowl and left. Monica came in, inhaled the fumes, and chlorine gas killed her. Vinegar mixed with laundry or household bleach also produced chlorine gas. The ME could probably determine on autopsy if Monica inhaled it.

Glass and window cleaners contained ammonia. Mixing ammonia with bleach produced deadly chloramine gas.

Hotel cleaning ladies undoubtedly used these products. I wished I'd asked Sara about them. She would know not to mix certain products, but how many others knew or read labels?

It was a wonder any of us survived to adulthood.

If the killer combined products, how could he protect himself from inhaling lethal fumes? He'd have to wear a protective face mask. Sam's officer had gone to Nix Hospital to learn about shoe coverings and booties. What about masks?

I searched the web for standard hospital medical supply forms. Several similar forms came up. I typed in "Hospital Supply Companies, San Antonio" and decided to go with the largest one, Axon Supply.

Using a computer program, I created an Axon Supply order sheet. It wasn't perfect, but I thought it looked legitimate enough to pass for a standard order supply form if nobody looked too closely. Everybody's mind was on Fiesta, which would help. It was only four thirty. I had time to go to Nix Hospital.

I blew my hair dry and decided what I'd wear tonight. For now, I put on minimal makeup and pulled on a nondescript outfit that could pass for business attire. Slipping the laptop into the case, I stuffed essentials into inside pockets so I wouldn't have to carry a bright fiesta purse. Clipping my order sheet to the clipboard I kept handy for "official" visits, I went down to the registration desk.

"Hello. I'm a hotel guest with a document I need to copy."

"Sure. Our business office is around there." He pointed to an office down the hallway left of registration.

"Thank you." Followed by the fragrance of gardenias, I scurried to the office, turned on my laptop, printed my document via the hotel printer and attached it to my clipboard. Back in the lobby, I spotted the concierge and asked for walking directions to Nix Hospital.

Taking Casa Prima's exit to the River Walk, I walked toward Arneson Theater. The open-air amphitheater built by the Works Progress Administration in 1939-1941 had tiers of concrete seats rising up one side of the river with the stage situated across the river. I'd absorb unique details of the venue later.

The top of the amphitheater steps ended at a street level entrance to La Villita, the city's original town and current arts village. From there, it was a six-minute walk to Nix Hospital.

Throngs of people roamed the streets dressed in vivid colors and crazy homemade hats decorated with Fiesta and Alamo City symbols. By contrast, the Nix Hospital lobby was quiet and dignified. I walked to the information desk.

"Hello. I represent your hospital supply company. I got a call the hospital needs to refurbish stock before Fiesta gets in full swing. I think they mentioned gowns and booties."

"That would be Sophia, second floor. But I'm sure she orders by phone. What did you say your name was?"

I slurred out, "Christina Gallegos, Axon Supply."

"Maybe I should give her a call." She started to punch a button.

"Not necessary. I have to make a doctor's appointment first. Then I'll pop by and see if she's still there. Thanks."

I walked briskly toward the elevator, stopped at the building directory and looked back to see if the girl at information was pushing buttons. She was watching me.

I shrugged. "I forgot what floor he's on." I ran my finger down the names. Administration Offices were on the second floor. Storage for hospital supplies was probably there. Doctor's offices were on floors three through six, and the hospital occupied the upper floors.

I finger waved the desk girl, gave her my sweetest smile, slipped into the elevator and pushed three in case she had a way to see where the elevator stopped. Exiting, I walked down the hall reading doctor's names on doors, considering how to find the supply room and what to say when I got there. A nurse darted out of an office and faced me. "Can I help you?"

"I was hoping to make an appointment." I looked sheepish. "I'm not sure which doctor I need."

She frowned. "What is your medical problem?"

"Uh. Well, you know, female problems." I tried to appear conspiratorial. My stomach growled. "And stomach irritation." Ignorant about anatomy, I figured it was all in the same general treatment area.

She looked perplexed. "Most urologists and gastroenterologists are on five. You might try there."

"Great. Thanks." I got back on the elevator and pushed the button.

When I stepped out, I was surprised to find the fifth floor full of people: men, women and efficient uniformed nurses.

I didn't relish bumping into the same helpful nurse on the elevator, so I decided to find the exit to the stairs and take them down to two. I thought it might be awkward to search for the stairway exit with so many people milling around, so I meandered into a doctor's office and plopped into a waiting room chair. I'd stall a few minutes until the floor cleared out. Patients straggled out of the office until I found myself the only one left in the waiting room. When I stood to leave, the receptionist caught me.

"The doctor is finished for the day. Do you have an emergency?"

"Oh, no. Just female problems."

She stood over her desk, leaned through the sliding glass window and studied me. "Dr. Probant is a urologist specializing in men. Unless you have a prostate gland, I don't think he can help you."

Face flushing, I managed to give her a cheesy grin. "I guess not. Have a nice day."

I fled the office into the vacant hall, clipped down to one end and got lucky. Pushing open the door to the stairwell, I pattered down to the second floor. Peeking out, I saw the entrance to a ladies' room across the hall and went in to powder my face and collect myself enough to appear business-like.

Back on the floor, I walked purposefully down the hall, trying to look official holding my clipboard while I scanned for the supply room.

Another nurse stopped me. "Can I help you?"

"Yes. Someone in supply, Sophia I think, called asking us to restock some items. I'm new with the company, so she asked me to stop in to make sure I order the correct items." I moved my clipboard to an angle where she could see "Hospital Supply" in large letters. The "Axon" name and logo were harder to distinguish.

"Supply is down there."

I nodded sweetly and scurried in the direction she pointed before she wondered why I came so late in the day. Peering through the top glass of the door she indicated, I saw an orderly checking off supplies, shelf by shelf. I knocked.

"Yes?"

"You needed supplies?" I held up the clipboard, opened the door and held out my other hand. "Christina Gallegos. I'm new with the supply company."

"Mike Cervantes. I didn't call, but come on in. Must have been Sophia. She already left."

"She said you might need more gowns, booties and other items with so many people in town for Fiesta."

"I was just doing inventory. Let's see what we have." He walked toward shelves that held green hospital gowns, booties, hair caps and masks.

"Plenty of caps. Everybody hates those." He counted hospital gowns and marked a number down on his sheet. "We could use three dozen more gowns. I hope we don't have an influx of patients over Fiesta, but we typically do."

While he counted booties, I made notes on Axon's supply list on my clipboard.

He picked up a bootie. "I can't believe people take these ugly things." He shook a full head of thick brown hair that could profit from a cap. "They pilfer them to cover their shoes if the weather is bad. It ruins the booties, of course. We're a little short. Hard to believe, isn't it? I'm always amazed at what people will take."

I nodded. "How many pairs do you need?"

"Well, patients never wear them. Three dozen should do it."

"Anything else?"

"Looks like we have a healthy surplus of everything. Let me count the masks...Hmm. Looks like we're a little short. Better send us four dozen."

"Can I see one? I want to make sure I order the kind everybody prefers." I felt the material.

"It's three-ply. Has melt-blown material between woven fabric which acts as the filter that stops microbes from entering or exiting the mask."

"We carry those." I jotted items on my board. "I don't know why anybody would take them home, though. They make it hard to breathe."

"They get used to them. People use them for spraying pesticides. Woodwork. Sanding. Painting. Sometimes docs coming out of the military request NIOSH N95 or N99 masks which block all air contamination." He handed me one of each. "Let's order a dozen of each."

"All right. I'll get this order in the system. You should have them in a couple days."

"Fine. Happy Fiesta."

"You too."

I walked back to the hotel, wondering how I was going to get gowns, booties and masks delivered to Nix Hospital.

Fifteen

Sam

Sam was glad Rick was the handling detective. He called him.

"Rick, this is Sam. Did you verify the complainant's current address?" He found it odd the police department referred to all victims as "complainants." Even dead ones.

"We did. She lived in MacArthur Park."

"Have you already gone over there?"

"Yes. Early afternoon. Complainant's house was empty. Neighbors weren't home. I left empty-handed."

"Okay. It's almost five. I'll go see if I can catch anyone coming home from work. Address?"

"134 Greenville Way."

"I owe you a big steak dinner."

"I know."

MacArthur Park included subdivisions bordered by Loop 410 East and Nacogdoches Road. Sam drove from downtown to Loop 410 and turned east. The park and surrounding subdivisions were named after General Douglas MacArthur, US Army Chief of Staff during the 1930s. Sam surmised his name drew Monica Peters to the area.

General MacArthur was recalled to active duty in 1941 after the Japanese destroyed US air forces in Hawaii and invaded the Philippines. As Commander of US Army Forces in the Far East and field marshal of the Philippine Army, he received the Medal of Honor for his prominent role in the Pacific theater during World War II. He also led the United Nations Command in the Korean War until President Harry S. Truman relieved him of his commands in April 1951 for making public statements which contradicted administration policies. His relief remained a controversial topic in the field of civil-military relations. Sam thought Monica would have been on MacArthur's side.

He looked at his San Antonio map and cruised until he found the right house. It looked like it might have two bedrooms. The small front porch was painted yellow and trimmed with white. The curtains were drawn and a lone light shone inside the house. Parking at the curb, he walked up on the porch and pushed the doorbell. He waited. No answer. He walked around the back of the house. Over the left side fence, he saw a neighbor's head retreat behind blinds.

Outside Monica's back door, a wrought iron table and chairs and colorful potted plants cozied a small concrete patio. Everything was well-cared for, but the plants were getting a bit dry.

A man from next door appeared in the yard.

"Can I help you?" the man said entering the yard. "I don't think Ms. Peters is home."

Hand outstretched, Sam walked toward him. "Detective Sam Vanderhoven, SAPD."

"Oh." The man looked surprised. "Harold Harper. We live next door."

Sam realized he wasn't in uniform. "Hope I didn't disturb you. Someone reported Ms. Peters missing and we're doing a preliminary investigation."

"I see. I hope she's all right."

"She probably is. It's Fiesta Week. She might be visiting a friend."

"This is my wife, Agnes. He motioned to the approaching woman who must have peeked through the blinds.

They appeared to be in their sixties. Harold wore a checkered short-sleeved shirt, striped Bermuda shorts and house shoes. His gray hair was thinning. Agnes' housedress was covered by an apron. She brushed flour off her hands and smoothed her hair. "Sorry, I'm baking a cake for our grandson."

"He's a lucky boy. I was just telling your husband someone reported Ms. Peters missing and we're doing a preliminary investigation. Do you know where she is?"

"I'm afraid not." They shook their heads.

"Have you known her long?"

"About two or three months. She bought the house after she left the Army. She's a cute little filly," Harold said.

"Flirtatious," Agnes said.

"How so?"

"She'd go out and talk to Harold every time he brought in the garbage can.

"She was just being friendly. A great neighbor."

Agnes pursed her lips. "She dated a lot of men. A couple of them stayed over."

Sam made notes and kept a bland expression. "How long ago was that?"

"Within the last month or two."

"Can you describe the men?"

"They were nice looking. One was in uniform," Agnes said. "Both had a military bearing."

"What branch of service were they in?"

"I don't know. I can't see that well." She straightened her spectacles.

"Did you notice what kind of cars they drove?"

"Each one had a car, but I can't tell one car from another."

"I didn't see the cars," Harold said.

"Do the men who visited live around here?"

"I don't think so," Agnes said. "They were younger."

"How young?"

"Probably in their thirties or forties. Hard to tell when a man's in good shape." Her eyes swept Harold's paunch.

Her husband grinned. "You checked out Monica's dates, huh, Agnes?"

She pursed her lips. "Teachers notice details." She turned to Sam. "I used to teach at Grove Elementary."

"What else do you remember about the men?"

"Not much." Agnes smoothed her apron. "She'd slip them in at dusk when you couldn't see much."

"Most young people have dates at night after work, Agnes. What were you doing?" Harold asked. "Hanging out the window?"

Chin raised, she thinned her lips. Sam pictured Agnes in front of her class.

"Of course not, Harold. I was tired of watching boxing matches and happened to look outside."

"I rang the doorbell," Sam said. "Do you know how long she's been gone?"

"I think about three or four days. I lose track," Harold said. "She stopped her newspaper and asked me to get her mail."

Agnes sniffed. "She would."

"I wonder if I could see the mail," Sam said.

"Sure. I picked it up today. Don't remember which other days I collected it."

Sam pulled a plastic bag from his pocket and dropped the mail into it. "Might help us know who she left with. Where did she work?"

"She was looking for a full-time job. She was good with computers, so she worked at home for clients she met in the military. I'm not sure what kind of work she did."

"Do you know if she took her car?"

"I don't know. Let's go look." They padded to the detached garage and looked through glass at the top of the door.

"It's a Honda," Harold said.

Sam recognized the metal curved above the trunk. "Looks like a Prelude. About 1995." That fit with what he thought Monica might be able to afford. "Nice car. She probably took a cab downtown to Fiesta. It can be hard to park down there."

"I think she did mention Fiesta," Harold said. "You'll be sure and return her mail to us, right?"

Sam nodded.

"I'm kind of worried about her," Harold said.

"Why is that?"

"Well, she lives alone. Looks vulnerable. She's a small woman. Sweet girl."

Agnes smirked. "Nice filly."

Sam wrote their names, address and contact information. "Thank you for your time. I'm sure she'll turn up." He didn't have the heart to tell them. "I might talk to your other neighbors. Who lives on the other side?"

"The McKutcheons. They're gone on vacation. Molly and Mason Sampson have the next house down. They have a bunch of kids and Molly's about the same age as Monica. You might try them."

"Thanks." He strode over the adjacent lawn, heard noise and kids in the next house and rang the bell. Molly came to the door, young, blonde, pretty and frazzled. He told her who he was and why he was there.

"Sure, come in. Monica mentioned going to Fiesta for a few days." He walked into chaos. Two young boys wrestled on the floor, a pre-teen girl moped on the sofa periodically screeching at the boys, and Mason Sampson tried to drown everybody out with TV football.

He squinted when Molly tried to introduce Sam, pushed himself up and reluctantly turned down the volume. "Why don't you kids go out back and play?"

The pre-teen girl looked offended. The boy who looked about eight moaned. "Aw, Dad, do I have to play with *them*?"

The redheaded boy about five yelled, "Beat you to the swing," and charged out.

"I'm sorry," Molly said. "Please sit down. Can I get you something to drink?"

"No, thanks, I won't be long. Somebody reported Monica Peters missing. We're checking the neighborhood and thought you might know her."

"We met her when she first moved in. I love to visit with Monica. She's funny and smart and loves life. Sometimes I go down there just to hear an adult voice and background silence."

Mason smiled. "Monica's a nice lady."

Sam turned to him. "Have you met or noticed anybody she dates?"

"No. When I get home about five, the kids are all over me and Molly's fixing dinner. After that we go to sports practice and help with homework before we crash."

"Is Monica really missing?" Molly asked.

"She might be at Fiesta, but it's been several days and her car is in the garage."

"I know she has friends from the Army. Maybe she's with them."

"Could be. Do you know their names?"

"I'm afraid not."

Red hair over a freckled face appeared at the back of the living room.

"She's real fun. She turns on music and dances around in the back yard. If I go over, she gives me cookies."

"This is our son Michael," Mason said.

"Sometimes she lies out there on a blanket without a stitch on," Michael said.

"Michael," Molly said, "you never told me that. You shouldn't be watching."

Michael's face turned somber. "She doesn't do it anymore. She's different."

"How is that?" Sam asked.

"She just sits on the patio with ugly clothes on and plays stupid music."

"I see."

"And she never makes cookies."

"Did she tell you why she was sad?"

"I just thought she didn't want to see me. So I left."

"When was that?"

"I don't remember. Last week. Maybe before Todd's baseball practice."

"That would be Wednesday," Mason said.

"Will you let us know when you find her?" Molly asked. "She's really become a friend."

"We will." Sam got their contact information, told them they had a beautiful family, thanked them and left.

They watched him get in the car and returned to their noisily happy house. Nice people. As soon as he got into the car, he called Detective Rick Montaya.

"I talked to some neighbors around Monica Peters' house. She works at home on her computer and her car is in the garage. Think we should get a search warrant?"

"I'm on it."

Sam shook the plastic bag and looked through Monica's mail. Bills and advertisements. Maybe they'd find somebody else's prints besides the mailman. "Monica Peters checked into the hotel alone, right?"

"Yep."

"The credit card she gave the hotel was hers, right?"

"Yep."

"Nobody used it since her death?"

"No. Her purse had everything intact and nothing new turned up. We'll have to wait on the crime lab and autopsy."

"Okay. We'll talk tomorrow."

He turned on the ignition and looked at his watch. Time to get ready to meet Aggie. She was being a good sport about the miniscule rooms. So far, so good.

Sixteen

Changing to Fiesta attire back in my room, my thoughts flipped to Monica. Assuming Sam was right and she knew the person who killed her, what could their motive be? Jealousy? Revenge over a perceived slight somebody suffered while Monica was in the military? Anger because she was leaving the hotel early? Anger because she told somebody she might be pregnant?

I could hardly wait to go on the River Walk with Sam. We would amble on concrete walkways banked by tropical foliage, meander past hotels, restaurants and shops and watch natives and tourists cruise the river on flat-bottom river barges. By crossing over river bridges, we could walk in either direction on both sides of the river. I'd walked it many times, always wishing Sam was with me.

I hadn't celebrated for years. After my tragic incident with Lascivious Lester, there was no reveling. I mistrusted men and spent my days numbly calculating figures at a Chicago bank.

When Sam's wife and daughter were killed in a traffic accident, Sam escaped to Texas to flee brutal winters and devastating memories. We couldn't even grieve together. But I never stopped thinking about him.

Chicago seemed progressively colder, and I wasn't getting any younger. After my bank stock skyrocketed, I had options. San Antonio seemed like a good place to start over.

Once Sam and I reconnected in River City, we saw each

other often over two years and grew increasingly close. I managed to confess that the daughter he raised and lost in the accident was my biological child. Unknown to Sam, his wife Katy and I arranged for them to adopt my daughter. By the time I confessed to Sam, he'd figured it out and forgiven me. We were starting over.

I took time with my makeup, donned a black cami and swirling lime green skirt and added dangling, beaded Fiesta earrings and beaded sandals. There was still time to check out the hotel shop before meeting Sam.

Meandering through the lobby, I gazed at display windows on my way to the shop. I peered into the restaurant. The Femmes were dressed and ready to party.

I swished to their table. "Y'all want to check out the gift shop before you go on the river?"

Phyllis pursed her bow-like lips in her round face. "I kind of hate to go in there."

Foxy swished her hand dismissively. "That was ages ago."

Martha Mayberry's wide smile stretched freckles across her nose. "I've been meaning to tell you, Phyllis, I *love* that little box purse. I'm too tall to carry something cute like that." Martha picked it up to admire it and the bottom fell open. A pill bottle rolled out and coins tinkled across the table. "Oh. The purse has a false bottom. How neat!" She caught the bottle before it rolled off.

Phyllis gathered the coins and took the pill bottle from Martha, fat tears dropping from her eyes.

"She's still worried about that silly shop. Forget it, Phyllis. The whole thing was a mix-up," Foxy said.

"I guess you're right." Phyllis dabbed her eyes. "It was embarrassing."

"You go ahead and shop, Aggie. We'll powder up and wait for the boys," Foxy said.

"Okay." The hotel gift shop was apparently a sore subject, which made me doubly eager to check it out. From curiosity, my feet started to itch.

The shop had an entrance off the lobby and another one to the River Walk. Entering from the lobby, I wandered around looking at goodies. The Femmes and boyfriends passed by outside on their stroll. "Have fun." I waved.

I turned to the clerk behind the display counter. "What a charming shop."

"We try to keep the best items," she smiled. Her brown hair was pulled back in a sleek bun. Dark eyes and thick lashes set off her skin the color of caramel cream.

"Aren't those the same lamp bases that decorate the rooms?"

"They're lovely, aren't they? And so heavy."

Between the lamp bases and small vases made in the same shape, sets of hammered silver tumblers sat on shelves.

"Those glasses would be beautiful in anyone's house."

"We sell a lot of those. They have dishwasher-safe liners and a treated silver coating that won't tarnish."

I thought about buying a set for Grace. Maybe it would cheer her up.

"We used to buy those glasses and other items from Foxy and her friends."

"I didn't know Foxy imported goods from Mexico."

"Yes, for a long time. We have several sources and buy from multiple suppliers."

"Being a few hours from Mexico, with cartels there and in Central and South America, I guess you have to be careful about ordering merchandise. You might get something in your shipments you didn't order."

"That can happen. We do have to be careful."

She was vague and trying to be professional. But Texas

shared a long porous border with Mexico. It didn't take a genius to imagine drugs smuggled in across the border.

Perusing other merchandise, I started imagining where drugs could be concealed. There were guayaberas in fine-woven cotton, Mexican and Guatemalan dresses and bright-colored blouses woven with multi-colored threads. Silver jewelry glistened in display cabinets. Leather-tooled handbags hung on display racks. Decorated wooden box handbags like the one Phyllis owned sat on shelves. It would be easy to pack smaller goods inside many items: lamp bases, vases, glasses and purses.

I was especially drawn to baby smocks from Guatemala, delicately embroidered with colored threads. "I love these baby smocks with the matching booties."

"There's a young woman who comes to Fiesta every year. She's fascinated with them."

She could be talking about Monica, unaware she was dead. "I see why she likes them. They're adorable. You have lovely items. I'll be back later to decide what to buy for a friend."

I thought I might find an item in the shop similar to a furnishing in the penthouse suite that could have been used to kill Monica. Sam said she had no marks on her body, so the killer might have used some common item that wouldn't draw suspicion, perhaps a receptacle that contained poison. The only shop items I recognized from the penthouse were hammered silver lamp bases. I hadn't seen any glasses. Of course, the killer could have brought a lethal substance in his own container and taken it with him when he left.

The baby smocks gave me greater sympathy for Monica. My conversation with the clerk created doubt about my new friends. I wished I hadn't seen a pill bottle and coins from Phyllis' purse roll across the table. What kind of pills were they? Investigating made me suspect everybody. I checked my watch. A little after six. I had time to do research before I met Sam.

Seventeen

I went back up to the fifth floor and headed for my cubbyhole. The hall seemed dead. I might be the lone person on the floor. I powered up my laptop, clicked on Internet Explorer and searched for Phyllis Morgan.

Phyllis finished high school in Houston and fell in love with a man who worked in the oil fields and was killed in a rig accident. Her work history listed several waitress jobs and a stint cleaning houses, which explained her empathy for Sara.

She enrolled in Junior College, studied to become a nurse's aide and apparently never re-married. She found work in a Houston hospital and somehow became assistant to the pharmacist.

Three years later, she moved to San Antonio. She had no current record of employment, but for a few months, she volunteered at Nix Hospital.

The article referenced Cenikor Foundation, so I scrolled to the bottom and clicked the link. Cenikor was a drug and alcohol rehabilitation facility that moved from downtown Houston to the suburb of Deer Park four years ago. President Reagan recognized it for its ability to operate without government funding. If Phyllis required rehabilitation, how could she afford such a place? Perhaps because of help from friends where she worked at the Houston hospital?

Musing about connections between Phyllis, her purse, the shop, her work at the Houston hospital, Cenikor, and her connection to Nix Hospital, I lost track of time. I glanced at my watch. Researching Foxy and Martha Mayberry would have to wait. I scurried down to meet Sam.

I found him in the lobby sitting near the river entrance. He'd changed to a Hawaiian shirt and pressed khakis. I wasn't sure where Hawaii fit in. Must be the shirt he thought looked most like Fiesta. He smiled and grabbed my hand as we walked outside. Warmed by the April sun and intoxicated with the sweet odor of Texas Mountain Laurel, it felt like we'd been liberated. This was how our days on the River Walk were supposed to be.

We walked on flagstones cemented together with grout. Raised, stone-banked beds against outside walls were filled with philodendron, banana plants, California fan palms, date palms, sago palms and colored with pentas. It was like we were in the tropics.

"I wonder who designed all this."

"Robert Hugman, a twenty-seven-year-old architecture graduate from the University of Texas. San Antonio reminded him of cities in Spain with narrow, winding streets barred from traffic. He viewed the river as a centerpiece with shops and restaurants on the banks," I said.

"Visionary."

"Yes." The sun turned orange, preparing to set, as partiers meandered beside the river. One girl wore an off-the-shoulder blouse with a six-inch drop ribboned with red and green ribbons. Her green cummerbund topped a skirt with horizontal strips of red, white and green fabric, colors of the Mexican flag. Lace separated the colors so the skirt flowed to her ankles. Her date wore a wide-brimmed Mexican sombrero topped with balloons and a replica of the Alamo.

Men and women in military uniforms meandered down the River Walk. I was glad Monica spent time on the river before she died.

"Does this river ever flood?" he asked.

"In 1921, a Gulf of Mexico hurricane dropped two to ten feet of water downtown. More than fifty people lost their lives."

"And people still wanted to beautify the river?"

"Hugman pressed anyone who would listen to his ideas. When the city started a flood control project, he thought they could construct a floodgate at the north end of the main river bend and a dam at the south end and isolate the river from flooding."

"So the city pressed forward with development?"

His brown eyes looked like they had deeper pools than the river. It was all I could do not to grab him right there on the river bank. But I wanted him to make the first move. He was the one who needed to be sure about our relationship. He grabbed my hand and stepped to the next flagstone.

"City officials thought a national firm should develop a master plan for the city and the river, so they hired a St. Louis firm. They pushed for a natural, pastoral greenway with no commercial development. By the time they and Hugman presented plans to city commissioners, the Great Depression was going strong. There was no money for either man's plan."

"That must have really discouraged Hugman. Let's sit a while."

We plopped on a bench, let walkers pass by and enjoyed the serenity of the lazy river. Lights strung from Cedar Elms, Lacey Oaks, Texas Red Oaks and Bald Cypress trees twinkled overhead and reflected in the water. I could sit there with Sam for the next thirty years. Or at least for several days. But he'd be absorbed with the investigation. I wanted to wait until I researched the other women to tell him what I learned about Phyllis.

"Isn't Night in Old San Antonio held around here?" he asked.

"It's in La Villita behind the Arneson River Theater steps. NIOSA is Monday and Tuesday night this year. Foxy said they changed the schedule to give the military time to get ready for the Cavalier River Parade honoring them on Wednesday night."

We rose and walked around the bend until we reached the Arneson Theater seats where patrons sat to view entertainment on the stage across the river. Rows of stone seats separated by grass curved upward in a concave arc toward street-level buildings and arches that led into La Villita.

I pointed up the steps. "These seats can hold a thousand people to watch a performance on the Arneson stage. The Femmes will perform there Wednesday night."

"That will be something."

"Let's climb the steps and go to La Villita."

With the river behind us, we climbed steps between the seats and paused under the arch at the top to peer into La Villita's patio. Food and beer booths were set up around the periphery in front of hundred-year-old buildings that housed shops. Swarms of volunteers decorated booths.

"With NIOSA starting tomorrow night, they're working fast."

"Maybe we can come," he said.

"I'd like that." The San Antonio Conservation Society sponsored and benefited from NIOSA. Hundreds of volunteers manned food and beer booths, and thousands more partied among the booths and enjoyed live music in the heart of the old town. La Villita was the "little town" that developed across the river from Mission San Antonio in 1809.

We went back through the arches, sat on stone seats and gazed at the river. Tree lights were brighter now. On the other side of the river, the Arneson River Theater stage lay silent.

"You know a lot about this River Walk," he said.

I smiled. "It's unique. I knew we'd be here together."

He emitted a sigh I couldn't interpret. "I'm glad to be down here. I've been too busy chasing criminals to take it in." He put his arm around my shoulder. "Tell me what happened with Hugman."

"The beautification committee collected money from businesses along the river and the city and secured WPA funding for the rest. After ten years, Hugman finally saw work begin on his River Walk in 1939."

"Hmm." He kissed me on the cheek. "So Hugman became famous and the River Walk grew and prospered?"

With him nuzzling my ear, it was hard to think. "Not exactly. When trees were uprooted, plants were destroyed and lots of stonework appeared during construction, the Conservation Society, the mayor and a hotelier's wife didn't like the way things looked. The mayor prompted Hugman to hire his cousin as landscape architect, but Hugman refused. The mayor cut Hugman's supply of rock to build river walls and bridges and redirected the materials to improve La Villita, which was also a WPA project. The river project was derailed."

"That was devious."

"It got worse. In March of 1940, the oversight committee fired Robert Hugman."

"He must have been devastated."

The image of Grace, sitting on the Sunbrella chair where I left her, devastated by Monica's murder, floated through my mind. I didn't tell Sam my thoughts. "Hugman *was* devastated," I said.

He shook his head. "Tragic."

He knew how tragedy felt. At that moment, he was probably reliving the pain of learning his wife and daughter—my daughter—were killed in an automobile accident. I had no remedy for tragedy. All I could do was try to move forward and wait for Sam to heal.

"At least most of Hugman's work had been done: stairways, walkways, the Arneson Theater and bridges. WPA denied attempts to change or remove completed features because they paid for them."

"That was some consolation."

I gazed across the river at the theater stage extending in an outward arc toward the river. Left of the stage was a simple stucco building with dark wood doors where performers entered to get backstage. At back center stage, three stone arches reminiscent of a cathedral rose atop a stone wall. Inside the open arches, bells hung from wooden crosspieces, two bells in outside arches and a single bell in the center. Palm trees swayed behind them. One large palm leaned over the arches from stage right as if protecting them.

"Hugman intended for bells to be hung in those arches, but after he was fired, he was ignored for thirty years. Finally, San Antonio's chapter of American Institute of Architects honored him publicly for the River Walk. While everyone else stood and cheered, Hugman cried."

"No wonder."

"In 1978, Lila Cockrell dedicated those five bells hung in Robert Hugman's honor. He was first to strike them and make them chime."

"It took so long for him to be recognized for his genius River Walk design," he said. "Sometimes justice comes way too slowly."

I took his hand and looked into his eyes. "You've spent your life trying to make justice work faster. That's something to be proud of." He smiled.

I liked to accelerate justice too. Since he didn't always appreciate my methods, I didn't mention it.

"Are you ready to walk back?" he said.

"Yes."

We went down the Arneson steps to river level and turned toward our hotel. Foot traffic was heavy now. We walked by anacacho orchids, Mexican olive trees and a scented lime tree. We wove in and out of people walking the other way, careful not to fall in the water. The river was only three to four feet deep, but if we fell in, we'd feel like idiots. The sweet smell of night-blooming Jasmine tickled our noses. Crotons grew near our feet.

Laughter echoed through the sparkle of overhead tree lights. Bouganvilla arched toward us from stone walls. We inhaled the sweet fragrances of angel's trumpet and confederate jasmine. A canna lily and rose of sharon sprouted by the river bank.

"This is idyllic," he said.

Ivy and potato vines hung from cracks in the stone walls. I inhaled the sweet aroma of wisteria.

"Are you hungry?" he asked.

"Yes."

"Let's see what they have in the hotel restaurant."

With so many choices on the River Walk, it's hard for hotel restaurants to compete. Sam seemed eager to get back. I just wasn't sure why.

Casa Prima's watering hole was practically deserted. I ordered a tuna sandwich and white wine but didn't eat the bread. After subsisting on MREs, real food tasted divine. He ordered scotch and water and a hamburger.

"Too bad they're not serving goodies in the penthouse lounge," he said, biting into the burger. When we finished, it was still early. He put his hand on mine. "Let's check out the view from up there."

Eighteen

We headed for the elevator. Since Sam had a standard key to his mini-room, he used a passkey the manager gave him to operate the elevator and open the lounge.

Inside the lounge, glass-topped tables curled around beige ultra-suede sofas to create intimate settings. Pink-toned light emanated from expensive lamps on Mexican pounded-silver bases.

On my trip here after seeing Monica, I'd been oblivious to panoramic photographs floating on the walls. The frameless scenes made it appear that pieces of San Antonio had drifted in.

A bird's eye view showed Casa Rio's colorful umbrellas shading tables by the river. Another photo showed charro dancers in twirling dresses filling the Arneson Theater stage. A wide-angle view showed the Arneson's stone seats we sat on overflowing with smiling tourists.

Photographs of San Antonio's five Spanish colonial missions from the 1700s hung individually to capture each one's distinctive beauty.

One entire wall looked like spring in bloom. A photograph of The McNay Art Institute stood in state on her magnificent grounds. Next to it hung scenes from the Botanical Gardens and Conservatory and Brackenridge Park with its Japanese Garden.

Images from Fiesta floated between scenes of the city. One showed a decorated barge with King Antonio and his aides standing regally in the bow as they floated down the river in the Cavalier River Parade.

My favorite panorama featured The Battle of Flowers Parade led by the band from Texas A&M University, the "Fightin' Aggie Band." Fiesta queens in elegantly beaded dresses rode on floats gliding between marching high school bands and pep squads. Blimps bounced against the sky. Military floats carrying beautiful girls and proud soldiers rolled along, the moving heartbeat of the city.

I noticed a huge skylight in the lounge ceiling, larger than the one I'd seen in the suite. Since it was nighttime, no light shone through. Yet I pictured Monica's illuminated face.

Sam walked to sliding glass doors that opened to a patio and slid them open. "Come stand here. You can see a lot of the city."

Buildings lit their facades for Fiesta. The river, with its tree-canopied lights flashing diamonds in the water, looked like a quicksilver artery pumping through the city.

He turned to me and smiled. Unruly hair, blown by the breeze, flopped against his brow. "It's hard to imagine anything happening here except celebration, isn't it?"

My urge to grab him competed with the sensation of falling. I felt light-headed, leery of tumbling off the balcony. My stomach was probably confused by receiving something besides MREs.

Oblivious to my condition, he planted his elbows on the rail and cupped his chin on his fists. "We don't think the killer entered Monica's room from the balcony."

I regained my equilibrium. Our potentially romantic moment dissolved into reality.

He looked around. "There's no way to scale these walls without being noticed. Thousands of people gather here during Fiesta Week. Anyone could have killed Monica."

"Aren't killers usually somebody the victim knows?"

"Statistically, yes." He turned to look at me. "What is it?"

"Even though Monica dated mostly military men, I can't conceive of one of them killing her."

"With four military bases here, plus Camp Bullis, Camp Stanley and thousands of veterans, it's possible."

"Harry Haddock said Monica dined with an Army officer. The Femmes said it was probably Hank Gleason. We can start there."

"I'll call Ft. Sam Houston's Commanding General. Maybe he can have somebody dig into Gleason's background." He leaned forward on the rail, looking dejected. "With crowds gathered at parades, and Fiesta events all over the city, someone could commit a crime, disappear into the crowd and leave the city. Or even the country. It would be hard to trace them."

My imagination ran wild. "You said the ME thinks Monica was poisoned with a liquid or gas. If somebody really wanted to cause havoc, they could drop something into the water supply or poison the river. Fumes would knock out people on the bank. We should have snipers on the roofs watching Fiesta events."

"Normally, I'd accuse you of having an overactive imagination. But I learned something earlier."

"What?"

"The mayor received an anonymous call. In a disguised voice, the killer said he was sorry to put a damper on the city's annual party. He told the mayor to enjoy the river during his last Fiesta."

It was hard to take it in. "The killer could be in this hotel. Someone actually staying here." I hated to tell him about Phyllis Morgan, her purse, her history with hospitals and the article reference to Cenikor, Foxy importing items for the hotel gift shop, and the manager's admission they had to be careful about incoming shipments, but I did.

"You're thinking the women could have smuggled drugs in?"

"I hate to be so suspicious, but it's possible."

"Cartels bring drugs into San Antonio in imaginative ways all the time, sometimes using unsuspecting carriers. It will be easy enough for SAPD to check drugs coming in through the shop and find out who was involved."

"It's hard to believe those women are capable of that."

He looked at me over his glasses. "Aggie, if you start snooping around and get into trouble, I can't protect you in this environment with everybody and his brother in San Antonio. You realize that, right?"

I nodded. I wasn't about to snap the last tenuous thread to our romantic rendezvous. I gazed out over the city. Whatever the killer planned next, it had to be tied to Monica. "I hate having to question Grace about Monica's private life."

"I know."

"Can the medical examiner tell whether Monica was pregnant?"

"He's starting the autopsy tomorrow. I'll call in the morning and tell him she might be. I think they can tell if a victim was pregnant, but it depends on how long she's been pregnant."

"What about blood tests, the toxicology screen?"

"That's looking for drugs. I don't know about pregnancy."

Monica being pregnant would be one more blow Grace didn't need. I walked into the lounge and sat on a sofa. He followed and sat beside me.

"We have to find out who committed this wretched crime," I said. "Did you learn any more from the crime scene?"

"Monica was apparently putting on makeup in the bathroom before she was killed. The techs grabbed the makeup, so the lab might find something."

"Could she have fallen and hit her head in the bathroom?"

"It doesn't look like it. She had no contusions, no bleeding from her head, no signs of struggle."

"What if the killer caught her before she fell, then dragged her."

"It's possible."

"She was dragged from the bathroom to the sofa, right?"

"We're pretty sure that's what happened from covered shoes moving backward followed by her dragging heels. But we're not sure where she was killed."

I decided not to divulge my trip to Nix Hospital. First, I wanted more pieces to fit together. "It's good that Sara vacuumed in the morning. It left the carpet smooth so drag marks were obvious." I had another thought. "Monica was very small. I doubt she weighed over a hundred pounds. Anyone could have dragged her. Even a woman."

He nodded. "Murder statistics show women are more apt to use poison. Men prefer knives, guns and arson."

I shuddered. Poor Monica. She was trying to get over a failed marriage and find happiness, dating men she thought were reputable. It didn't sound like she was happy, deciding to leave Fiesta early. And then to be murdered.

If she was pregnant, Harry Haddock could be the father. Or Hank Gleason. Or one of the men Sara saw enter her room. One of them could have killed her. If the Femmes were smuggling drugs into the gift shop and Monica found out, one of them could have killed her.

I sighed. "If she was pregnant, it should at least help us find her killer. I need to go to my room. I might have Dear Aggie letters to answer."

"I should turn in too. I have a lot of work to do tomorrow. I'll call you after the autopsy."

We rode the elevator down together. On five, he walked me to my door.

"It was a great evening, Aggie." He kissed me until my innards tingled. Then he drew back. "I'm sorry our rendezvous is ruined. I'm too caught up in this murder to feel romantic."

"I understand. Me too."

"Maybe as we get closer to solving this crime, we'll feel more normal."

Whatever that was.

"We'll have our time, Aggie. Sleep tight."

He headed for the elevator to descend to his lair. I had a momentary vision of him flipping in the twenty-seven-inch bed and landing on the floor. I giggled before I realized he might hurt himself.

Then I thought about Monica strewn across the sofa, probably pregnant with a life that also didn't have a chance. I no longer felt like giggling.

Nineteen

I brushed my teeth and put on my Garfield sleep shirt, but I wasn't the least bit sleepy. I sat at the desk, powered up the laptop and checked my email, hoping Grace or the newspaper sent me a letter to Dear Aggie.

My column originally began with ideas for staying young—guidelines for shaping up and tips for style and makeup. But I learned people's success in those areas was tied to their situations and relationships and their view of them. Optimism was a package. Exercise, good grooming, self-esteem and a tendency to expect the best were intertwined. There was a letter in my inbox.

Dear Aggie,

This is the most private, heartfelt letter I've ever written. My name isn't really Allison. That's just a happy-go-lucky name I like. I'm anything but that. My problem is I'm desperately in love. My parents saved money for years so I could go to college, and I have two years to go. I'm crazy about Mike (not his real name, either). I love everything about him, the way he talks, walks, smiles. I want to have sex with him. It seems so natural. I know he's the right man. He wants to go to graduate school, maybe law school.

He's bright, and I think he should go. He'll honor me by waiting to have sex if that's what I want. But I'm so tempted. What if he goes away and has sex with somebody else and falls for her? My friends don't think having sex is a big deal. I know how to avoid getting pregnant. But what if it happens accidentally? Birth control isn't foolproof. I might not be able to finish school. His education would be delayed. He'd have to go to work to support us. We could probably never even take vacations. I want to do this right. This is an important event in my life. I don't want to mess it up. But I'm so tempted. Send advice.

Agonizing in Alabama,
Allison

I leaned back in the chair and thought about my life. My getting pregnant with Lester wasn't my choice, but what if it had been? I'd thought I loved him and wanted to spend my life with him. My pregnancy changed my future. I could no longer make decisions for myself. I was now a woman with child, caregiver, provider, parent. My plans, my work, my education, my life were now predicated on what another person needed. Lester wasn't ready to follow the path he unthinkingly took in a passionate moment, wasn't ready to care, provide for or consider any other person, including me.

We thought our sex was love, but love was short-lived. Sex was temporary pleasure. For him. That wasn't how either of us planned it, but in our haste, we reduced it to that. It was like a climax scene in a movie. We didn't know each other, understand each other, honor each other or commit to each other. Or to the life we might create.

My tragedy occurred twenty years ago. When the pill

changed everybody's viewpoint, women were set free to do what they wanted. Or were they? Could I choose the right words to help Allison?

Dear Allison,

Of course, you're tempted. You're in love, and sex is a natural, strong, powerful urge. If it wasn't, our human race would dwindle out. But you're so much more than your urges. Your thoughtfulness proves it. You are hope, integrity, caring, loving, giving, intellect, faith, soul and promise. Develop these qualities for yourself and give him time to develop his. He may say he can't bear the thought of going away without having sex with you as his most treasured memory. If I had a quarter for every time a guy told a girl that, I'd be richer than Bill Gates. He might go away and have sex with somebody else, but that won't make him fall for her. You will be in his mind. And your sexuality won't go away. It will grow stronger because you will bring to it the sum of who you are. Look for admirable qualities in Mike. Search out his facets until you understand where each one fits in his life. He is much more than the way he talks, walks and smiles. If you find out he isn't, you haven't lost much. And you haven't diminished who you are. You friends say it's no big deal. What if your friends are wrong? Pregnancy aside, what can you lose? Does premature sex have destructive power? He'll never honor you in the same way. He can never be sure you were his first lover or that he'll be your last. You'll miss sharing what you've learned on your separate paths of experience. You'll miss watching him change and develop. Men change a lot between age twenty-two and twenty-six. They become very different people. You'll change too. Odd as it seems, after people marry, they rarely grow much. It's a fact. They stay pretty much the same. They're no longer inclined to reach higher or stretch further. Check with psychologists. You and Mike will both miss the joy and honor of sharing your bodies with each other for the first time. Not a small thing. What a gift. A permanent gift that grows and grows. If you thought sex had no real meaning, you wouldn't have written me. You know sexual intimacy is a major step. Integrity is knowing the right thing and doing it. Do you expect him to have integrity? Develop yours. Your struggle is more than worth it.

Agonizing with you,
Aggie

Twenty

There was no way I'd be able to sleep. Dredging up my personal agony to help Allison woke me up. Despite his saying he forgave me, could Sam ever commit himself to me? There might be one good thing about having to solve this horrible crime. My relationship with Sam was on hold.

I decided to go down to the restaurant and bar. Maybe I'd find some happy person to talk to, or I could just sip and think. The lobby was nearly empty. I heard people laughing and reveling on the River Walk, which added to my misery.

I peeked into the restaurant. At a table near the bar, I saw the pair Valerie interviewed in the penthouse, a handsome couple in their fifties. They could've been celebrating an anniversary. They looked up and smiled while I walked near their table. Fine lines appeared in the delicate skin around the woman's eyes. Her blonde-streaked hair was pulled back in a silver clip that matched her dollar-sized silver earrings. She looked classy and sweet. Her husband probably adored her. He had a high forehead, intelligent green eyes and gray slivers in his hair. Whatever kind of work he did, I sensed he did it well.

I paused. "I love your earrings. Did you buy them around here?"

"Thank you. Yes, I found them in a shop on the River Walk." Her smile lighted her face.

"I think I saw you being interviewed in the penthouse by Officer Garrett. My fiancé, Detective Sam Vanderhoven, and I were supposed to have a room there...the one where the tragedy occurred." I liked calling Sam my fiancé. "He's working on the case."

"How awful for that to happen," she said, lines forming in her brow.

He stood and offered his hand. "We're Connor and Anne McVey. Won't you sit down?"

"Thank you. Aggie Mundeen."

"Will you join us for a nightcap?" Anne said.

"How nice. Yes. Chardonnay, please." Connor motioned for the waiter and gave my order. Through the restaurant's plantation shutters, I saw Live Oak leaves fluttering in the breeze. I longed to be on the River Walk, but not alone.

"From what little I saw, the suites must be beautiful."

"They are," Anne said. "We've been building a business, and Connor's been working nonstop. We decided it was time to take a break, come downtown and act like tourists."

I sipped the drink, comforted to sit and relax with nice people. I contemplated my situation. If I stayed, I needed to formulate a plan to learn more about Monica and people she knew to ferret out her killer. Or I could give up investigating, let Sam do his job, go home to my bungalow and try to ignore my itching feet.

"Tell me about your suite," I said.

"The living area is spacious," she said, describing a room like the one I'd seen. "And the bathroom is huge."

"Towels are twice as thick as ones we have at home," Connor said.

"The bedroom colors are so inviting. The bed and comforter feel like clouds," Anne said. Connor smiled at her.

We talked about Fiesta and upcoming events.

"This was our first opportunity to be together," I said. "Since Sam is a detective, he has to investigate the case. Hotels are all booked, so our time together is ruined. I'll always wonder how it would have been to stay in a suite like that."

"I remember meeting him," Connor said, "and I saw him walk you to the elevator." They looked at each other, understanding passing between them.

"I imagine the suites are all the same," Anne said. "We're not going out tonight. Would you like to look at ours, just so you'll know?"

"We're happy to show it to you," Connor said.

My face broke into a grin. "At least I'll have that to remember."

Their living room had the same ultra-suede sofa and glass-topped tables that appeared to float in the room. Stout pieces of carved furniture, strategically placed to draw attention to their solid beauty, offered contrast. The room looked larger when my attention wasn't glued in horror to the sofa. Weak city lights filtered through the skylight. Lamps glowed with a flattering pink hue. Across the room, tied-back drapes revealed a balcony.

Anne followed my gaze. "You can see the river from there."

Sam said there was no way Monica's killer could enter the room through the balcony without being seen. I walked over for a closer look. The balcony was four feet deep, barely wide enough to hold two metal chairs and a small table. No one but Spiderman could scale the wall and get to this balcony. Not far from the hotel, a curved section of river wound beneath the trees.

"We don't sit there. We can't see enough of the river. We'd rather be down on the River Walk. Come see the bathroom," she said.

Thick taupe towels engraved with Casa Prima's initials draped over heated bronzed-gold towel bars. Beige tiles covering the floor were scarcely visible under a three-inch-deep ecru shag rug. From the shower and tub, the rug ran up under the sink cabinet and snaked around toilet fittings. No one's feet would have to touch a cold floor. Bronzed-gold fixtures in double sinks matched those in the shower. Sconces with identical finishes flanked the mirror. Two simple recessed light fixtures blended with the ceiling. One was on. In keeping with the elegant décor, a single wall switch operated the lights.

"Exquisite. It makes you want to stay here for the bathroom alone."

"Doesn't it?" Anne said, walking into the living room.

I saw three room keys in the bathroom makeup tray, slipped one in my pocket and followed her out.

Connor had settled on the living room sofa.

"I was wondering," I said. "Did you know the dead girl?"

They shook their heads.

"Did you hear anything from the hall?"

"We arrived Saturday evening," Connor said. "We had dinner and asked the bellboy to take our luggage to the room. We were tired and went to bed early."

Anne put her hand on Connor's arm. "We heard that commotion Saturday night."

"That's right. I heard shouting, went to our door and looked out. A man burst from a suite into the hall, and somebody slammed the door behind him. He looked embarrassed when he saw me, plastered a smile on his face and mouthed 'Sorry.' I thought he might have had a spat with his girlfriend. When I met him later, I was surprised to learn he was the manager."

"Harry Haddock?"

"Yes. We were introduced when he was up here with the police after the girl was killed."

"Which room did he come out of?"

"I'm not sure. It was the middle of the night, and I was half asleep. It could have been the victim's room or the one next to it. I wasn't sure, so I didn't want to get him in trouble with the police. I thought as the manager, he might have a plausible reason to argue with whoever was in there."

"I understand." Sam said Monica told Harry on Saturday night that she intended to check out Sunday. They fought. It escalated...

"Did you tell the police later?"

He shook his head. "I should have. I'll tell the detective first thing tomorrow."

Anne nodded. "After breakfast this morning," she said, "we strolled the River Walk, ate lunch and came back for a nap. Next thing we knew, the police were beating on our door. Poor girl. I can't imagine anyone killing a young woman."

"I can't fathom it either."

"Do you want to see the bedroom?" Anne asked.

It looked larger than the one in the suite Sam and I would have shared. A high-backed leather chair studded with metal brads stood by a small round table in front of the window. I hadn't seen a chair in the crime scene bedroom. Maybe my viewing angle wasn't right. Plus, I was in shock from seeing Monica.

A massive closet spread across the interior wall. Opposite the foot of the bed, a closed cabinet most likely held the television. Plush pastel linens covered the bed. With daylight from the window, there was no need for a skylight. The McVeys had tossed bright pillows onto a chair.

I pictured having dinner with Sam, then going upstairs to a penthouse suite. Our luggage would be there. The lights would be dim. We'd change into lounging pajamas. I doubted he had lounging pajamas. He probably didn't know they existed. Oh, well. It would be a long time before I had the opportunity to luxuriate in a space like this.

"Thank you for letting me see your room. It's nice to know what he planned for us."

"Our pleasure," they said, grasping my hand before I turned toward the door. I felt terrible snitching an extra key from these gracious people, even though I had a reason.

"First thing tomorrow," Connor added, "I'll tell the detective about the manager's outburst."

"Good idea. Please don't mention you showed me your room, though. It'll just make him feel bad. He's working long hours to solve this crime. I don't want him to know how eager I was to see a penthouse suite."

"We won't mention it. Good night."

I stepped out into an eerily quiet hall.

Twenty-One

Nothing stirred. I listened for sounds. There were none. I tiptoed down the hall. Police had put a "Do Not Enter" sign on the crime scene suite and removed the yellow tape. I noticed a new sign on the door to the penthouse lounge and inched toward it. "The lounge is closed. Penthouse patrons are invited to enjoy Happy Hour at the lobby bar."

Since the standard key to my cubbyhole wouldn't open the lounge, I'd snitched the McVeys' extra key so I could enter the lounge to study the bathroom. Right now, I was more interested in the door midway down the hall marked "Employees Only."

I looked both ways and didn't see anybody. No sound came from the rooms. This was the best time to check the maids' storage closet for cleaning products. If anyone got off the elevator and saw me, I'd act like a confused person trying to get into the wrong room.

I thought about Sam's admonition not to snoop. How dangerous could this be? I was in the penthouse of a luxury hotel in downtown San Antonio in the middle of Fiesta. All I had to do was scream and a dozen people would show up. Monica must not have screamed.

Since my cubbyhole was usually reserved for staff, I hoped the standard key they issued me would open the "Employees Only" storage closet. I guessed right. The door opened.

Cleaning supplies filled the shelves: vacuum cleaner and bags, dust rags, furniture and metal polish, Windex, ammonia, toilet bowl cleaner, tile cleaner, light bulbs for lamps, pillows and blankets, toilet paper rolls, tissue boxes, soaps and toiletries.

Next to the vacuum cleaner were two vertical boxes. I pulled them out and opened the taller one that pictured a skylight tunnel. I found a lens cover, rim and a three-to-five-foot extendable metal cylinder, a tunnel to the roof. I replaced the items, put back the box and opened the second one. It contained a standard recessed light fixture with a housing for the bulb and a lens cover and rim identical to the one for the tunnel skylight. I replaced the parts and put back the boxes. I looked again at light bulbs on the shelves. Most were soft three-way bulbs for lamps. Others would fit in the housing for recessed ceiling lights.

I heard the elevator open, backed out and swirled around to face Harry Haddock.

He stormed over, walked up close and squinted down at me with his hand on the open door frame. My back was against the door.

"A little late to be getting toiletries, isn't it, Ms. Mundeen? On the penthouse floor?"

"I needed a few things for my cubbyhole. I thought they might have prettier soaps up here. Larger. Better shampoo." Before my reasonable self had time to take over, I took a deep breath and spilled out words.

"Somebody heard you and Monica Peters screaming at each other in the middle of the night Saturday, heard her slam the door and saw you blast out of her room."

I wasn't positive it was him and Monica, but the odds were good. I was in so much trouble already, I might as well go for it.

A series of expressions passed over Harry's face. The first one was anger.

If I poked his eyes and kneed him in the groin, could I beat him to the fire stairs and scurry down far enough to get away before he could recover?

His angry expression morphed into thoughtfulness. He might be considering the ramifications of my being Detective Sam Vanderhoven's girlfriend.

"The detective is bound to find out you and Monica were shouting. If he hears it from me, he'll be less upset. You don't want him to find out you lied."

His eyebrows tented into forehead wrinkles. He sighed. I thought he might have decided to tell the truth. He dropped his hand off the door frame and stepped back.

"I knew Monica. We dated whenever she came here. I liked her. But she dated so many other people, it was frustrating. She always stayed for a week. This time, she booked for ten days starting Thursday night. We usually don't make such long bookings during Fiesta Week because people change their minds. But for her, well, I did it. We had dinner Saturday night. About one o'clock the assistant manager called me for an electrical emergency."

I noticed he didn't say what they did between dinner and one a.m. Maybe he made a move on Monica, and she rebuffed him. Maybe she thought she was pregnant and told him. And the baby wasn't his.

"After I took care of the electrical problem and went back to her room, she informed me she was leaving Sunday. Just like that. No reason. No explanation. Just Adios. She hadn't prepaid, so I knew I was stuck. We could probably rent the room, but we might not be able to coordinate nights with other guests who wanted rooms for more days. Those penthouse suites are expensive."

What other jilted boyfriend would worry about room occupancy except a hotel manager? I gave Monica a mental high five for ditching this one.

I tried to look sympathetic. "You were furious."

"You bet I was. I yelled at her. She yelled back, threw me out and slammed the door."

"In a rage, you came back and killed her."

"No! I'd never do that. The detective can check my whereabouts the rest of that night and the next day."

I was glad to know he was still thinking about Sam. Those mental calculations might have saved my life.

"I'm sure the detective will check your whereabouts. I'm meeting him for a nightcap. I'll put in a good word. Next time you see him, it'll be better if you don't mention our conversation. Mind if I get some soap?"

"Take all you want." He glared at me as I scavenged through goodies. I selected three perfumed bars, two large bottles of shampoo and conditioner and facial tissue and hustled toward the elevator. Even if Harry wasn't Monica's killer, I didn't think it was prudent to stick around.

Twenty-Two

I woke up at seven thirty, groggy from watching scenarios flit across my brain. I had a suspicion Monica was murdered in the bathroom of her suite, but my ideas about the method were vague and unsubstantiated. Once I put the pieces together, I'd tell Sam everything.

I needed breakfast by the pool. I donned a pink cami and swirly multi-colored skirt to wake myself up and get into the Fiesta spirit. I hid my duplicate key from the McVey's room in the recesses of my suitcase for later use.

At the pool, I found a perfect spot in the sun, slid onto the chaise and caught the waiter's eye to beg for coffee and order breakfast. I flipped my phone open to call Sam, inhaling the aroma of coffee emanating from the cup clasped in my other hand. "Good morning. What are you doing?"

"Morning." He sounded wide awake and professional. "I'm working on drugs coming in through the hotel shop. The Drug Enforcement Administration confirms what we already knew. Since we're a hundred and fifty to two hundred and fifty miles from storage points at Mexican border towns, dealers break drug shipments into smaller packages there for smuggling into the US. We're talking cocaine, heroin, methamphetamine, marijuana, and MDMA—molly and ecstasy—and even ephedrine and pseudoephedrine tablets. Immigration and Naturalization recently found cocaine inside boxes in a tractor-trailer mingled with a shipment of t-shirts. One supplier sold HCL gas to Mexican methamphetamine producers along with solvents and reagents. We have the honor of being near the border where the majority of drugs come into the US. There's no doubt small drug shipments are distributed through here. I'm going to check connections between drug arrests and this hotel. You?"

I described my nightcap with the McVeys and summarized what they said about Harry. I didn't mention visiting their suite, snooping in the hall closet and getting caught by Harry. The McVeys would tell him all he needed to know.

"I'll have a chat with Haddock and verify his every move between Saturday and Sunday when we found Monica," he said. "Once I get the ball rolling on the drugs, I'll get all I can on Hank Gleason. Then I'll go to the ME's building for the autopsy and check with the crime lab. I'll call you. What are you going to do?"

He apparently accepted the fact that I wasn't going to stand idly by and do nothing. "I might look for the Femmes. Their boyfriends were in the Army. Maybe I can learn more about Monica."

"You won't do anything foolish."

"Of course not. I want to stop by and see Grace. NIOSA is tonight. Why don't we go?"

"You're staying, then?"

"Tonight, anyway. We have to go to at least one Fiesta event."

"I'd like to. We'll see how today goes."

I was devouring a cinnamon roll and sipping Casa Prima's delectable coffee when John, Roger and a gorgeous man in uniform came from the hotel into the pool area. The soldier was tan and fit with stripes and medals pinned to his shirt over muscles. Roger wore a bunch of medals, but this soldier was the real deal. They looked around, spotted me and strolled over.

"Hello, Aggie."

I swallowed coffee, sat up straight and produced my best smile.

"This is Major Hank Gleason," Roger said. "We were all stationed at Ft. Sam Houston together."

"As you can see by his medals," John said, "Hank stayed longer. But Roger and I have a long history there. When our fathers were stationed there, they were friends."

"That's impressive."

"Yeah," Roger said, "tough old birds. They're lying in rest at Ft. Sam Cemetery."

I extended my hand to Hank. "Aggie Mundeen. It's nice to meet you. I've seen so many active duty servicemen but haven't had the opportunity to talk with them. Did you happen to know Monica Peters?"

"We had dinner once. The guys told me what happened. They dated her too. What a tragedy."

Roger nodded. "Nice girl."

"Hard to comprehend something like that," John said.

"I'm sorry I didn't know her better." Hank Gleason had blue-violet eyes and dark, thick lashes. If he kept smiling, I could look at him forever. How well did he really know Monica? It would be easy for her to fall hard looking into those eyes.

They were distracted by a girl in her twenties who strolled past in a bikini striped with Fiesta colors with a gigantic purple paper flower pinned in her hair. They gaped.

"Nice flower," Roger said.

Hank attempted to elevate the conversation. "I enjoy the Army," he said, "more than these guys did." He shrugged. "There's nothing wrong with becoming a civilian, though."

"Honorably discharged, at your service," Roger said.

"Currently proud employee of the San Antonio Water System."

I remembered the killer's words to the mayor, "Be sure and enjoy the river for your last Fiesta." Did the water system have any connection to the river?

Hank glanced at John. "A general discharge is good too. You served your country and landed a good job in the metal plating business, right?"

"For a while. Then I went into roofing. As a kid, I'd climb on roofs with the roofers. Got whipped for it a lot. I recently formed a company that installs solar panels. It's the going thing. Pays more."

"We always had a hard time keeping John's head out of the clouds," Roger said.

When they laughed, Hank produced another high-wattage smile.

John looked at his watch. "The girls might be waiting in the lobby. They want to do some shopping and scope out the Arneson River Theater."

"Are you dancing with the Femmes, Aggie?" Hank asked.

"No, but I might watch them rehearse."

His wattage increased. "If you decide to join in, I'll look for you in the lineup." He turned and followed the other men out, prepared for the heat with their water bottles with floating lemon slices. If I had to perform somewhere and Hank the Hunk was in the audience, I doubted I could remember where my feet were.

None of the Femmes mentioned that Roger and John dated Monica. Counting Harry Haddock and Hank Gleason, there were four men who could have gotten Monica pregnant. And four who could have killed her.

I finished my goodies and went back to my cubbyhole. The men's discussion of Army discharges made me curious about their backgrounds. I wanted to browse the internet.

Honorable discharges like Roger received were self-explanatory. General discharges could be honorable or OTH, other than honorable. A general discharge under honorable conditions meant the member's service was satisfactory but not meritorious. He might have engaged in "minor misconduct or received non-judicial punishment." Since Hank said John had a general discharge but secured employment at a plating company, his infractions in the military, if any, must have been minor.

A service member receiving a general discharge, OTH, displayed a pattern of behavior which significantly departed from expected conduct, like violence, illegal drug use or disrespecting a superior. This person was barred from re-enlisting in any branch of the armed forces. They were entitled to VA medical and dental services, home loans and burial in national cemeteries but couldn't receive educational benefits. If they searched for work or applied for school, an OTH attached to their discharge could have negative consequences.

Military personnel files were accessible only to service members and people they designated. I didn't want to probe Phyllis and Martha about their boyfriends.

This was a good time to see Grace.

Twenty-Three

Sam

Sam decided to call General Dayton, Commanding General at Ft. Sam Houston Army Base. He'd met him playing golf with SAPD Chief of Police, Ray Brigham. They all hit it off, played together at Ft. Sam Houston and the San Antonio Country Club and were equally mediocre players. Sam never mentioned their friendship at work. He knew he'd get a lot of suck-up kissie noises.

He called General Dayton's office and spoke with his assistant.

"Just a minute, Detective Vanderhoven." He put Sam on hold, then came back on the line. "He's here now. I'll put you through to his office."

"How are you, Sam?"

"Hello, General. Thanks for taking my call. We have a problem downtown in one of the hotels. A suspicious death, probably a murder. I talked to Chief Brigham. He hoped to play it down to keep from disrupting Fiesta, but once the ME rules her death a homicide, I'm sure it will hit the newspapers. The victim was stationed at Ft. Sam and discharged from the Army a few months ago. Her name was Monica Sheridan Peters. I wonder if you can tell us anything about her service."

"I'm sorry to hear that. I can have someone look up her record."

"That would be very helpful. We're also interested in Major Hank Gleason, active duty."

"Currently stationed here?"

"Yes, sir."

Sam could hear the General writing. "We'll add him on. I guess you need this yesterday?"

"Yes, sir, I'm afraid so."

"I'll get somebody on it. When are we going to play golf?"

"I don't know. In a month or so, I hope. I'm sure Chief Brigham will call you."

"You both better practice. I'm determined to beat you guys. I'll get back to you."

"Yes, sir."

Sam's next call was to Harry Haddock. He waited for Haddock to come on the line. "Mr. Haddock, this is Detective Sam Vanderhoven." He heard Haddock catch his breath. "I'd like information on one of your guests."

"Oh." Haddock cleared his throat. "Uh, sure."

"She's with the Fabulous Femmes convention. She might have booked rooms for the group. They call her Foxy."

"Ms. Strong. Used to be Mrs. Howard Strong. What would you like to know?" Sam heard Haddock clear his throat again. He sounded nervous.

"For now, just her full name and address."

"If you hold, I can get that right now." He came back on the line. "It's Felicia Finnegan Strong, 12749 Winding Canyon Road, San Antonio, 78261. That's somewhere out near Stone Oak, Canyon Springs or Cibolo Canyons. Anything else?"

Haddock tried to appear helpful, but Sam sensed the manager wanted to get rid of him. "Not for now. I might have you come down to police headquarters later to discuss your statement. I'll let you know."

He had one more call to make.

"Law Office of Stanley, Person and Shanks."

"This is Sam Vanderhoven calling for Burton Stanley."

"Yes, sir. I'll put you through."

"Sam, how's the law enforcement business?"

"About as busy as the divorce business. Can you find out how much money parties got in a divorce settlement?"

"If the parties entered into a property settlement agreement, it might not be part of the public record. But if one sued the other and a judge determined the division, the property settlement is public."

"Okay. The parties were Howard Strong and Felicia Finnegan Strong, San Antonio, divorced, I think within the last couple years."

"I've got a paralegal at the courthouse now. We'll see what we can find."

"Great, Burton. Thanks."

Sam couldn't think of more calls to make. He exhaled and looked at his watch. Time to go to the autopsy.

He drove to the Medical Center. Rick Montaya would be there. He questioned why it was necessary for detectives to routinely attend autopsies. They might glean some lead from the complainant's clothing. Mainly, they were there to hear the doctor state the cause and manner of death, which they usually knew already. In this case, it was critical information.

He parked at the building housing the Bexar County Medical Examiner's office. The crime lab occupied the upper floors. He entered and was about to push the elevator's down button when Rick walked into the building.

Sam held the door. "Anything new?" he asked Rick.

"Not yet. I went to Nix Hospital and checked out the shoe covers. They're flimsy. If that's what the killer used, we should have seen fibers in the carpet. Maybe Evidence picked some up. We can check with the crime lab when this is over."

They pushed the button to the basement. The lower the elevator descended, the more it smelled like a meat market. Morgues were put in basements in areas nobody saw. When the elevator stopped, an assistant greeted them. Sam wondered how the guy could work there. They walked past a walk-in refrigerator where the recently departed lay.

"They're about to start, Detectives. You can suit up."

They put on hospital scrubs and disposable plastic gowns with long sleeves. They put on shoe covers, hospital hair nets and masks with see-through panels that covered their eyes in case something splashed. The thought of it made Sam gag. The assistant had them don three layers of rubber gloves.

The diener had wheeled the body into the autopsy room and double-checked her identity. They had removed her clothes and put them on another table to pack up and eventually return to SAPD. The diener followed Sam's gaze. "We saw pressure marks under her armpits as though someone might have carried her."

Dr. Fortunas greeted them, one of four forensic pathologists who performed autopsies for the medical examiner, another job Sam would never want. "Let's get started, gentlemen."

The autopsy room had long metal tables attached to large sinks. The girl lay on the center table. He looked away from her pale, lifeless face. She looked altogether different from when he first saw her on the sofa. When the diener, the autopsy assistant, started working on the body, Sam studied the room.

Buckets on shelves contained specimens in formalin, a formaldehyde preservative. Aging anatomy posters hung on tile walls. The pungent smell of formaldehyde combined with odors of bleach and disinfectant reminded him why he never liked biology lab.

Fortunately, fewer autopsies were performed now than in

the past. Computed tomography (CT) and magnetic resonance imaging (MRI) scans took a lot of the mystery out of why someone died. But for unexplained deaths, complete autopsies were still necessary.

When the diener got to the pelvic area, Sam asked the doctor about her being pregnant. Dr. Fortuna probed around and finally gave Sam an answer.

It seemed like an eternity before the pathologist stated that the cause and manner of death were "pending analysis."

He looked up over his mask. "I suspect this girl was poisoned. But we won't know for sure until we get the chemical analysis back."

Twenty-Four

Albatross took me from Hildebrand to North New Braunfels. I turned right on Burr Road and approached the Ft. Sam Houston golf course, thinking about seeing Grace. When my phone rang, I pulled to the curb and stopped.

"You were right," Sam said. "Monica was pregnant. If they have reason to suspect it, the pathologist looks at the uterus for the site where the fertilized egg implanted. He found it."

"There's no doubt she was pregnant?"

"None."

"Has she been pregnant for a while?"

"He said she had to be two weeks late on her period for him to find the implantation site. She could have been pregnant longer than that, but that was the minimum. He suspects she was poisoned, but he can't determine what caused her death until he gets back the chemical analysis."

"I see." The timing of her pregnancy fit with what Monica told Grace. I hoped the painful knowledge would help us find her killer. Knowing she could have been poisoned made me feel worse.

"Are you going to see Grace?" he asked.

"I haven't decided."

"Okay. I put out feelers about Hank Gleason and Foxy's divorce. We can catch up later."

I started Albatross, rolled down Burr Road and slowed

before Grace's house. After hearing Sam talk about Monica, I wasn't up to seeing Grace. I passed by her house and mine and sailed past Ft. Sam Houston's golf course.

I didn't have any military men in my family. My parents died when I was young, and Aunt Novena and Uncle Fred raised me. Yet, for some reason, ever since I arrived in San Antonio, I had the urge to go on base. I thought about everyone's ties to Ft. Sam: Monica and three men who dated her, Hank, John and Roger. Since the last two had fathers buried at Ft. Sam Houston National Cemetery, maybe I could glean a few tidbits about their backgrounds. I'd absorb the news about Monica and seek some peace.

I drove to Harry Wurzbach Highway and turned left. A couple blocks ahead, yellow blinking lights marked the entrance to Ft. Sam Houston National Cemetery. Stone columns topped with urns flanked the open wrought-iron gate. Not thirty feet inside, an endless sea of headstones marked lives and deaths of thousands of men and women who served our country. The road continued to a 1940s vintage stucco building with a red tile roof. I parked in the small parking lot and walked toward a sign near the building. "We preserve these hallowed grounds with dignity, pride and honor. We will provide service to the veterans and their families with professionalism and compassion."

I climbed five steps to the building's small front porch where a kiosk held a machine and the sign, "Enter a name to find a burial site."

The front door to the building opened. "May I help you?"

"I'm looking for two service men I think are buried here."

"Do you know their names?"

"I know their sons' names."

"Let's see what the machine tells us." We walked over to it. The screen showed letters of the alphabet. "The son's last name?"

"Plunkett."

He punched in letters and a series of names appeared.

"Roger Henry Plunkett," I pointed. "That has to be his father."

"Okay, then." When he pushed the name, a printed sheet appeared. "Let's see where he is. "

The sheet listed Roger Henry's date of birth, death, interment, US Army as branch of service, highest rank held—Major General, the section of cemetery where he lay and number of his burial site. He was the right age to be Roger's father.

"I see Roger's dad was a high-ranking officer. Are officers buried in a particular place?"

He chuckled. "No. We assign them to an available grave space after receiving report of their death. There's no preference for rank, sex, or religion. They all served our country. For our benefit."

"Indeed they did. Can I find his grave by the section and site number?"

"Yes. Let's have a look at the map."

Numerous sections spread east from Harry Wurzbach: grave site sections, committal shelters and columbaria. A faint line on the map extended outside the marked areas of the cemetery.

"That line indicates land the government owns where other service men and women will be buried. We have over three hundred acres, enough space, we hope, for the next seventy years."

"How many thousands are buried here?"

"About eighty-three thousand veterans with wives and families."

"Are loved ones buried near their veteran?"

"They're buried with them. Original graves were nine feet

deep and accommodated three or four family members. Now they're not so deep, but we can bury them side by side." He smiled. "They're together."

"Are you in the service?" I asked.

"A grateful volunteer, William Johnson."

I smiled and extended my hand. "Aggie Mundeen. Can we look up another name, John Abbott?"

We walked to the porch. He punched "Abbott" into the machine and several names appeared.

I pointed to John Fielding Abbott. "I think that's it." He lived from 1930 to 1995, the correct age to be John's father.

"He was also a Major General," he said.

"Their sons are friends."

"Isn't that something. Since they died within a few years of each other, they're most likely buried in the same area, Section Eleven." He reached for the map. "I'll show you how to get there."

I went back to the entry road, headed east and stopped at a tall plaque to the right of the road. It was Abraham Lincoln's address when he dedicated the first national cemetery at Gettysburg. "We have come to dedicate a portion of that field as a final resting place for those who gave their lives that our nation might live..."

I drove to a roundabout circling a landscaped area with a tall flag in the center. Left of the circle, I saw the marker "Section Eleven." I parked and walked into a field of headstones. The grass under my feet felt sacred.

From a side view of the first headstone, rows of markers beyond were straighter than any fence. From any angle, headstones were perfectly aligned. "We cannot dedicate—we cannot consecrate—we cannot hallow this ground. The brave men, living and dead, who struggled, have consecrated it far above our poor power to add or detract..."

Walking through rows was peaceful. The sun shone, and a gentle breeze ruffled spring bouquets placed on graves. I felt like waves of headstones protected my path. I heard TAPS playing in the distance.

I consulted my paper. Roger Henry Plunkett was at site #2361. I saw a headstone with flowers and hoped it was his. I walked over.

Roger Henry Plunkett
Texas
Major General
United States Army
Korea
1926-1997

*A soldier proud
to serve his country.*

He died at age seventy-one. He and his wife were buried together. Her name was on the back side of the headstone:

Alice Amanda Plunkett
1928 – 1996

*Faithful wife to
her beloved warrior.*

Roger Plunkett lost his mother two years ago and his father only last year. No wonder he had flowers on their grave. Circling the bottom of the plastic vase, replicas of Roger's Fiesta medals lay alongside the medal of a skull.

A grave several rows over also had flowers. I found the graves of John Abbott's parents.

John Fielding Abbott
Major General
United States Army
Korea
1930–1995

*Here lies a great and
dedicated warrior.*

Both men served in Korea, another tie binding them and their sons. The other side read:

Maria Castaneda Abbott
1940–1975

His wife.

Maria was ten years younger than her husband and died at age thirty-five. Her inscription, short and impersonal, made me wonder about their marriage. Below the vase holding their flowers was a small pin, a skull.

I sailed back Burr Road past our houses. I couldn't face Grace until I had something positive to say.

On my drive downtown, I thought about connections: John and Roger, their officer fathers, their mothers, warriors' wives. Had the sons lived up to expectations of their high-ranking fathers? How did their mothers influence their view of women?

I thought about Monica enlisting and dating NCOs after her discharge, flirting with Foxy's husband, then dating only officers. Did the same man who killed her impregnate her?

I thought about her yelling match with Harry Haddock. I pictured Hank Gleason, made for the military, gorgeous in his uniform, dating Monica, Foxy and countless other women.

I wanted to trust my new friends, but I couldn't ignore Foxy's connection to the gift shop. Did she conscript the other girls as unknowing carriers for illicit drugs? Did Monica find out? Were these women totally different from how they appeared? All these people touched in connecting circles. They had all touched Monica. And she was dead.

Twenty-Five

As I snaked my way back to Casa Prima, traffic was getting heavy. The closer I got to downtown, the more people milled through streets wearing Fiesta finery and laughing. Excitement crackled the air.

Fortunately, the hotel still had room in the garage. I showed my ID to the officer at the hotel entrance and started across the lobby. Everything looked normal. I peeked into the restaurant and saw Foxy, Phyllis and Martha about to sit at a table. Since I knew where they were, it was a good time to check in at the gift shop.

The dark-eyed beauty with caramel-crème skin stood behind the counter. Otherwise, the shop was empty.

"Hello, I was in here the other day admiring your hammered silver glasses."

"I remember."

"Are you the manager?"

"Owner/manager. How can I help you?"

"I'm still interested in the glasses, the ones Foxy used to bring you from Mexico."

"Have you decided to get them?"

"Yes." I fished for my credit card. "I'll take eight sixteen-ounce tumblers."

She wrote up the purchase and starting wrapping each glass individually.

"The other day, you mentioned you have to be careful about

unwanted items in your shipments. I wondered if you ever found anything to report to police."

"Yes. They questioned a number of people, including me."

"And Foxy and her friends?"

"I imagine so. I never asked." She lowered her eyes and kept wrapping.

"Nothing comes smuggled in with merchandise now?"

When she looked up, her gaze was direct and pointed. "Police said they found the culprits and jailed them. Problem over."

"I see. Well, that's good to know. I'm sure my friend will be delighted with the glasses."

She handed me the package. "I'm sure she will. Stop by again."

I smiled and turned to exit the shop. I could feel her eyes tracking me into the lobby.

Foxy, Phyllis and Martha were still eating in the restaurant. I joined them and ordered the daily special so it would arrive quickly.

"I shopped all over the River Walk, remembered these and came back to buy them." I unwrapped a glass and watched their reaction.

"I've always loved those glasses," Martha said. The others nodded.

"They do carry intriguing things," Phyllis said, her cherub face paling before it widened around a smile.

"It's a great shop," Foxy said, expressionless.

If they had any further reaction to the shop or the glasses, it didn't show.

"Where are the guys?" I asked.

"They're working today," Phyllis said, "so they can take off early tomorrow when we rehearse. We're going to NIOSA later tonight. Want to go?"

"Sam and I might go."

"Maybe we'll see you there," Martha said.

I took the elevator to five and slipped inside my burrow to power up my laptop. Sleuthing in the storage closet gave me an idea. I wanted to do a quick internet search on skylights.

The first skylights I found were the kind one usually thinks of: holes in the ceiling, two by four feet or larger, with a sleeve extending up through the attic that ended at a skylight cut into the roof. A plastic or glass dome would be placed on the roof and sealed to capture the sun and send light into the room below. The cover could be hinged to raise and lower to let in air as well as light.

Smaller skylights, like the one boxed in the storage closet, were called sun tunnel skylights. A picture of them showed ten-to-fourteen-inch openings on roofs covered with clear glass or plastic. Light passed through tunnels down to the ceiling where a concave piece of glass, held in place by a plastic or metal rim, lay flush with the ceiling.

The glass and rim visible inside the room looked exactly like the trim on a recessed light fixture. I could imagine Sara confusing skylights with recessed lights and forgetting to install bulbs.

It was amazing how much light tunnel skylights let in. One with a fourteen-inch roof opening could light a four hundred and fifty square foot room. A ten-inch square opening on the roof could illuminate a room ten by nineteen feet.

I was beginning to form a hazy picture of how Monica could have been killed, but I couldn't pinpoint how it was done, why she was killed or who did it. Sam reported the pathologist said the cause of death was poison, inhaled or ingested. How was Monica poisoned?

My research revealing Phyllis Morgan's experience with hospitals, pharmacies, and her connection to the rehab facility were troublesome. Yet I couldn't fathom her smuggling drugs. It was hard to imagine her sweet round face hiding something that evil. I hoped Sam found the truth.

I searched for Martha Mayberry. Born in El Paso, Texas, Martha Hansen married Adolfo Mayberry at age eighteen. They had two children, Chris and Selena. Adolfo rose to manager at Builders Supply Depot and was transferred to Laredo. To supplement their income, Martha worked in gift shops in Laredo and Nuevo Laredo across the Texas-Mexican border. After the children graduated high school, Martha and Adolfo divorced. She moved to San Antonio and worked in gift shops at North Star Mall and River Center Mall. I found no reports of her being fired or having a criminal record. But she had experience with gift shops and frequently changed places of employment.

Felicia Finnegan Strong, Foxy, had married twice but had no children. She had eloped with her third husband, wealthy widower Howard Strong. Following a three-year marriage and nasty divorce, she ended up with a three-karat diamond ring, a saucy personality, an aggressive nature and a propensity to take charge. After her divorce, she had no record of employment. She either received a chunk of Howard's estate or found another lucrative avenue to support herself.

My fun-loving new friends could make my Fiesta sadly more memorable.

I needed to escape my cubbyhole and party. We had already missed St. Mary's University's Oyster Bake, Sunday's Mariachi Mass at San Fernando Cathedral and undoubtedly other events I didn't know about. I didn't want to miss another minute. I called Sam.

"Let's go to NIOSA. It's a perfect time. People don't expect it to start tonight, so there'll be smaller crowds. If we go soon we can scope out shops in La Villita and have a look at the Arneson River Theater."

"I'll meet you in the lobby in thirty minutes."

Twenty-Six

I put on a gauzy, ruffled fuchsia blouse, flared skirt, earrings that looked like bundles of curly ribbon and gold sandals. Sam was waiting for me at the entrance to the river.

The River Walk was crowded with people. Food smells drifted from restaurants. Fiesta was in full swing.

When we reached La Villita, the patios teamed with partiers. Shoulder-to-shoulder people in bright clothes adorned with Fiesta medals careened happily between food stands, beer booths and shops. Two men with loud shirts wore wide-brimmed Mexican sombreros. On top of one sombrero, flowers circled a mule piñata wearing his own sombrero. His friend's hat held dancing girls and plumbed birds. Another girl, wearing an off-the-shoulder white blouse, had a cartridge belt around her waist over her short skirt. Her long legs stretched into cowgirl boots.

Some revelers bought cascarones, hollow egg shells filled with confetti, to crack on each other's heads. In the background, musicians played "Feel So Good."

The Conservation Society held NIOSA in La Villita every year. The little city, now a historic arts village, was San Antonio's original neighborhood.

"Let's go to the shops first. How about Casa Manos Alegres, the house of happy hands?"

He smiled and nodded. We were glad to be together, away from work. I wanted it to last.

As we entered, a bell rang on the door. A sea of colorful products from San Antonio, Mexico, and Central and South America covered every surface. We admired Ken Edwards stoneware and lingered in front of Ecuadorian beaded necklaces, earrings, belts, purses, wristbands and hair bands. Embroidered Mexican floral dresses hung in wall niches along with embroidered baby dresses like the ones in the hotel shop. Papier-mâché ornaments lay on tables, and Papier-mâché piñatas hung overhead.

Displays of various sized skulls caught my eye, skulls disembodied from their skeletons. I thought about the skulls on the graves of Roger's and John's parents.

Skulls were made into jewelry. Others were made of plaster with jeweled eye sockets. Larger ones were drawn on t-shirts. A few were large enough to hang on the wall. Why would anyone decorate with skulls?

I asked the lady behind the desk. "Can you tell me about the skulls?"

"They're for Day of the Dead celebrations. Families remember deceased loved ones with decorations and food. They beautify alters with items the family member liked. Sometimes they embellish graves and have parties at the cemetery. The skulls represent the dead."

I was fascinated. I knew the Catholic Church, some Eastern Orthodox Churches, and the Anglican Protestant Church honored the dead in the fall on All Souls Day and All Saints' Day.

"Don't churches honor deceased loved ones in November? This is April."

She shrugged. "People prepare all year long. We always have calls for calaveras—skulls."

I glanced at Sam. His jaw was set. I walked over to him. "What is it?"

"The shiny thing on the table you noticed by Monica. It was one of those skulls made into a pin," he said. "The pin was wiped clean of fingerprints."

"Let's get some fresh air."

We walked outside and stood on the porch, not ready to descend into the crowd. We smelled tortillas, beans, cheese and beer. Sweet smells of lechequemada and calavasate candy drifted by.

Sam was thoughtful. "I've been asking around about the skull and about Day of the Dead. Seems it's a popular holiday in Mexico that made its way here."

"Why would Monica Peters celebrate Day of the Dead?"

"That's what I wondered. The skull pin might have been part of her Fiesta collection. But if it was hers, her prints should've been on it. We think somebody placed the skull pin on the table because it meant something to him."

"I'll go online later and see what I can find. When I talk to Grace tomorrow, I'll ask her if Monica ever mentioned the Day of the Dead celebration."

"Good. Let's see if other shops carry skulls."

Villita Stained Glass had sun catchers, kaleidoscopes and original glass designs made into bevels, prisms, and treasure boxes. No skulls.

Angelita's, housed in a one-hundred-year-old building, had beautiful linen clothing, hand-loomed sweaters and crafts. Shirts with pleated fronts that hung outside trousers reminded me of the guayabera Roger Plunkett wore. Angelita's didn't carry Day of the Dead artwork. They referred me back to the first store.

A shop housing the Starving Artist Art Group featured jewelry, pottery, wood and metalwork, original work by thirty artists and craftsmen. Sales benefited the Little Church of La Villita, the non-denominational church in the center of the village.

I picked up a brochure about the church and read high points to Sam. "Rev. John Wesley DeVilbiss, a Methodist circuit-riding preacher and volunteer missionary, rode horseback into the Republic of Texas in 1842. Two years later, he held the first Protestant worship service in English for a small group of Christians. Worshippers built the church in 1879. The church's mission, to serve the poor, still continues."

Wanting to see the little Gothic revival church, we ventured into the crowd. We made it to the church steps and gazed up at wooden double doors with cathedral-shaped glass inserts. Slender arced windows flanked the doors and continued around the sides of the narrow building. With the crowd shoving us back and forth, it was hard to stay in front of the church.

Someone called my name. "Aggie! Over here!"

I turned to see Phyllis and Martha with their boyfriends waving me over. The tallest thing I saw was Flamboyant Phyllis' hat, the one John Abbott made for her out of miniature solar panels. I grabbed Sam's hand and headed for Phyllis' tower. From a center pole two feet high on top of her head, small solar panels hung at rakish angles. Phyllis squinted with concentration.

It probably took a lot of focus to keep her tower upright with panels flopping around her head and bodies bumping against her. She must really love John to wear the rakish tower. At least it made her tall enough to stand out in the crowd. A tag with the name of John's company flapped off to one side: "Let Light Into Your Life. Call SINFULLY SOLAR."

Every time somebody bumped against her or John, he'd fumble around and hand them a company card. He looked like he'd had several drinks, so fumbling took longer than usual.

Before he could say "Thinfully Tholer" and plant a card on them, the moving crowd swept away prospects.

Madhatter Martha's sunflowers were still glued on, but her garden had tilted. Her boyfriend, Roger Plunkett, wore a different guayabera laden with medals. I eased closer to see them better.

The official 1998 Fiesta San Antonio Medal pictured people frolicking on either side of a miniature river under a blazing sun. Roger's Fiesta medals included ones from the Fifth Army, Ft. Sam Houston, Lackland Air Force Base, Joint Services Military Medals and the Military Civilian Club. He had this year's medals from King Antonio and from Rey Feo, San Antonio's other Fiesta king who raised the most money for scholarships.

Roger's large yellow button highlighted this year's Battle of Flowers Band Festival, sponsored by the same women who founded the original Fiesta parade and Texas History Oratorical Contest.

Roger's torso was covered. Sam and I, fascinated, drew closer and squinted at his chest. Nestled among the medals was a small pin, a skull.

"Do you celebrate Day of the Dead?" I asked.

"Not really, but it's part of San Antonio's culture. I thought I should include it."

"Where did you buy the pin?" Sam asked.

"Geez. I don't know. I've been collecting these things for years."

"You have wonderful military pins," I said.

"I was discharged with a medical disability. Now I work for the city water system, SAWS. I guess I'm a medal hound. I like to find 'em and trade 'em."

"You betcha," slurred John. He touched his own medals. Unlike Roger's, they were haphazardly pinned. "Medals make you feel like some kinda General, don't they, Roger? It's a lot easier to get medals that way than to earn 'em in the Army, right?" He attempted to pat Roger's shoulder and swished air.

"Sure."

"I like your medals," John slurred. "Even if they're not the real thing."

"Hey. You were both military brats," Phyllis said. "We should go, John. This tower is giving me a headache."

"Yeah. I'm getting thirsty." He aimed for a beer booth.

We heard a woman squawk on a loudspeaker and turned away from the foursome. Onstage, Foxy boomed into a microphone, effusively welcoming everyone to NIOSA. We gravitated toward her. She must be an officer in the Conservation Society that sponsored the event. As she rambled, the crowd grew louder and ignored her.

"Are you getting hungry," Sam asked.

"Yes. Something over there in the corner smells divine." We nudged our way toward the booth, making slow progress as the crowd pushed us side to side. As we were herded along, somebody spilled beer on me. I brushed it off and couldn't see who did it. We neared the booth. I smelled the odor of cooking beef and saw fajita meat on a stick. I was starving. We were almost there when the grill sizzled.

White steam rose from the patio around the booth and mushroomed into a fog. We couldn't see and lost our sense of direction. Nobody could see. Revelers grew disoriented. Murmuring voices held tinges of panic.

I spied the arch over the Arneson Theater entrance and grabbed Sam's hand. "Let's go sit inside the theater."

He took the lead and pushed through the crowd.

"What on earth is that fog? It doesn't have an odor."

"It looks like dry ice people use in stage productions. I don't know why anybody would use it here."

We had almost reached the arched entrance when I felt a

prick on my shoulder. I looked back, startled to see a man wearing a skeleton mask. The smoke screen obscured the rest of him.

"Don't you like medals? Viva Fiesta!" He pinned a skull on my shoulder and disappeared into the crowd.

Sam drew me under the arch. "It's another one of those Day of the Dead pins." He unpinned the medal and looked around. "Where'd that bastard go?"

"We'll never find him in this chaos. Let's just go."

We reached the Arneson Theater seats. I took a deep breath. "That's a terrible prank to play in the middle of NIOSA."

"Yeah. If that's what it was."

Twenty-Seven

We sat on a concrete seat near the top of the theater.

"That's way too many people," he said.

"And too many drunks. I smell like beer. What do you think happened with that cooking smoke?"

"Probably an accident. Somebody might have spilled something on the grill," he said. "Cleared out the crowd, though."

In the patio behind us, musicians played "Show Me Love." We had a wonderful view of the sparkling river. Tourists ambled along the banks. From around a bend, a river barge filled with sightseers floated by with a guide describing points of interest.

"Those are Yanaguana River Cruises," I said.

"The barges are so quiet." We could barely hear the motor.

"In their river cruise contract, Yanaguana agreed to provide boats powered by compressed natural gas instead of gasoline so they'd be quiet and not produce fumes. Hugman originally pictured gondola rides. They were used first to ferry passengers. That's why people call the city 'America's Venice.'"

"We need to take one of those cruises, Aggie. Maybe when all this settles down."

After seeing skull pins on graves, on Roger's shirt, and having some creep in a skeleton mask pin one on me, it didn't look like things would settle down soon. Seeking calm, I gazed back at the river.

A soft breeze rippled the water. Willows bent lazily with the breeze. People wandered up and down, smiling and laughing. I wished Sam and I were as carefree. "Do you think that man pinned me at random? Or was it some kind of warning?"

"I don't know. We need to learn more about this skull thing."

"I'll research it. I saw more of them today at the cemetery."

"The cemetery? What made you go there?"

"Hank and Roger, the Femmes' boyfriends, came to the pool this morning with Hank Gleason, the Army Major the Femmes and Monica dated. They're all part of the circle who touched Monica."

"Okay."

"Hank Gleason is still in the Army. The others were discharged, Roger with an honorable discharge and John with a general discharge. I wondered about their military backgrounds. I didn't want to probe the Femmes about their boyfriends, so I researched Army discharges. John's general discharge indicated his service or conduct wasn't up to par, or at least not commendable. It could carry a stigma when he tried to get a civilian job."

"I see. I'll investigate his employment after discharge. What else?"

"Service personnel records are private, but since their fathers are buried at Ft. Sam Houston Cemetery, I went there to see what I could learn. It's amazing. With nothing but somebody's last name and a few facts, you can find somebody's grave. Volunteers help you find it in a sea of thousands."

"And?"

"Both their fathers were Major Generals. Their sons have known each other for years. I wondered how their fathers' military status affected them."

"So we're back to what the men did after discharge."

"I think John owns his solar company, so we wouldn't have a boss or reference to check. But before that, he worked for a roofing company."

"We have a list of contractors we call to work with SAPD. We'll look for a roofer who installs skylights and solar panels and see what we can dig up about John's company."

"He previously worked for a plating company. San Antonio must have several. I'll check the telephone book and visit one tomorrow."

"Good idea. Better make it early. Some businesses close early for Fiesta. Rick can ask a patrolman to go with you."

"I think I'll get more information if I go alone. Just a curious tourist asking questions."

"That's probably right."

"Roger Plunkett got an honorable discharge. Did you hear him say he works for San Antonio's Water System, SAWS? I wonder if SAWS is connected to the river authority."

"Are you still thinking somebody could poison the river?"

"I know it's implausible, but consider this: the pathologist says Monica was poisoned. The killer who called the mayor either killed Monica or knew who did, and specifically mentioned the river. With so many people here, this nutty person could delight in causing havoc to the water supply or the river."

He thought about what I said. "Aggie, if you run into anything suspicious, I want you to call me. No snooping in dangerous places."

"I promise."

I gazed at the glittering, slow-moving stream winding through the heart of the city, drawing innocent revelers to its banks.

"I think we should concentrate on what we know and follow those leads," he said.

"All right. Tonight, I'll research Day of the Dead. Maybe pinning a skull on someone is part of celebrating Fiesta, like cracking cascarones on people's heads. It would be nice to know if I was celebrated or targeted."

"Sounds good. Let's get back to the hotel. We've had enough excitement."

I couldn't disagree.

It wasn't the kind I originally anticipated, but I liked the way we were working together.

I stopped and looked at him. "Any of those men or Harry could have impregnated Monica."

He nodded.

"Is it possible to check DNA of the four men against DNA found on Monica?"

"If they found semen, it is. We were focused on her pregnancy. As far as I know, they didn't find semen. The problem is, even if one had sex with her and the pathologist found semen, we can't demand these men submit to cheek swabs to check their DNA. We need some other reason for tying them to her murder. Then we can take a swab. Since the McVeys heard Haddock fighting with Monica, we can haul him in and test him. For the others, we need evidence."

We strolled home under pecan trees and Arizona ash. I stopped to smell a rosemary bush in the beds and admire the ferns.

We passed two women wearing black wide-brimmed sombreros trimmed with silver pom-poms, San Antonio's Spurs basketball team colors. Silver feathers burst from the tops of their hats around spurs glittering in the center. Their dates wore Spurs team shirts. The foursome painted a good picture of the togetherness Fiesta and the Spurs brought to the city.

"The Spurs won the first-round NBA Western Conference Finals over the Phoenix Suns," he said. "They lost to the Utah

Jazz the second round, but they'll win some NBA championships down the road."

"You might not have been to the river, but I see you're up to date on the Spurs."

Neither of us was hungry. We took the elevator to five, and he kissed me at the door with an urgent sweetness.

"We'll solve this thing, Aggie. Then we'll work on solving us." In his grin, I saw the same doubt and hope I felt. He gave me a hug and headed toward the elevator.

I took a shower, washed my hair, blew it dry and got ready for bed, pulling on pajama pants with my Garfield sleep shirt. No need to be glamorous. I was too tired to research anything and fell into bed.

Twenty-Eight

The next morning, I placed my laptop on the desk. While I waited for it to power up, I thought about people who didn't like Monica. Her ex-husband, for one. But I doubted he followed her to Texas to kill her. Foxy didn't think much of her. I thought it was jealousy, which was a long way from murder. Unless Monica discovered she was smuggling drugs. Monica seriously ticked off Harry Haddock.

Flamboyant Phyllis and Sara Giles both liked Monica. Martha Mayberry seemed neutral. She seemed to like everybody. I should talk to them again as well as Grace. One of them might remember another person Monica knew or dated.

It was time to research Day of the Dead. I found that rituals celebrating dead relatives dated hundreds of years back to the Aztecs. The custom spread and melded with other traditions.

In Mexico, the day was a public holiday. Family members placed departed one's favorite foods and beverages along with photos, memorabilia, sugar skulls and marigolds on alters as ofrendas, offerings. Sugar skulls were gifts for the living and dead. Marigolds were called flor de muertos, flower of the dead.

People decorated loved one's headstones and danced around them so that cemetery gatherings became parties.

The family's intent was to encourage visits by departed souls, so the souls would hear prayers and comments the living directed to them. Roger and John could have placed skull pins on their parents' graves as a communication portal.

Some parties included pranks. The man who pinned the skull on me at NIOSA—did I remind him of a departed relative? Did the skull have any relation to the identical pin found near Monica? Was I designated to be the next departed soul? Chills raced over me.

I had no previous connection with Monica, nor did Sam. But we were supposed to move into her room after she left. Did someone resent us, thinking we were somehow to blame for her decision to leave, and make sure she couldn't leave?

Searching the internet, I found pictures of skull pins made into lapel pins, broaches, cufflinks, tie-tacs and tattoo art. Skulls were nestled in flowers, made into pinup girls and carved in antique ivory. Being pinned by a stranger in a skull mask at NIOSA might be some sort of compliment.

Was the fog of dry ice at NIOSA a prank or a method to cover the identity of the masked man who pinned me?

I clicked to "Uses of Dry Ice for Halloween" and learned how to make witches brew with sherbet, lemon-lime soda and dry ice in a cauldron. Hot water poured over the ice created a fog. Viola! Witches brew.

If you set a tall glass inside a carved pumpkin, poured it half full of hot water and salt, placed dry ice around it, poured hot water on the ice and covered the top of the pumpkin, white smoke flowed out through carved openings. Somebody at NIOSA blended Fiesta with Day of the Dead and Halloween. I was probably the random bystander of a Fiesta prank.

I put on calf-length white chinos, a black t-shirt, sexy black sandals and a ton of silver jewelry. Feeling spiffy, I strolled across the lobby to the restaurant. I was surprised to see the girls there so early. Foxy was mesmerizing Phyllis and Martha with whatever tale she was telling. I decided to join them.

"Good morning." Phyllis and Martha looked better without a solar tower and sunflowers weighing them down.

"Have a seat," said Foxy. "We just got here."

"What did Sam and I miss at NIOSA last night after the smoke went away?"

"Nothing, really," Foxy said. "The bands stopped playing for a while, but once the white smoke cleared, everybody went back to partying. I can't imagine why anyone would play such a stupid prank."

"John and I left as soon as we could see. He'd already had plenty to drink and was scheduled to check solar panels this morning. It gets hot crawling over roofs. Makes him grumpy. I hope he doesn't fall off. He makes good money, but I liked him better when he worked for the plating company. At least he wasn't always on edge. Literally."

Martha piped up. "He sure was cranky last night about Roger's medals."

"I'm sorry about that. It was the booze talking."

"Roger loved the military," Martha said. "He enlisted. He would have stayed in, but when he showed up with a heart murmur, they discharged him with a medical disability. Coming from a military family, he was devastated."

"No wonder he loves military medals," I said.

She nodded.

"He's very proud of his service. The medals make him feel like he's still part of it. He goes all out for Fiesta Week. Thank goodness he has a steady job with SAWS."

"John loved the military too."

"He was discharged?" I prompted.

"About a year ago." She didn't elaborate.

"Did any of you know the military man Monica Peters dated?" I asked.

"Sure," said Foxy. "Major Hank Gleason. Monica didn't

date NCOs. Funny how the least likely people turn their nose up at somebody else."

Phyllis looked disgusted, but she'd already defended Monica. Martha just shook her head. They must be used to Foxy's critiques.

"We all dated Hank," Martha said. "Even Foxy."

"Well, who wouldn't?" Foxy said. "He's so gorgeous."

"I met him," I said. "I agree. I guess Roger and John dated Monica too?" I wanted to see what they'd say.

"Briefly. Before she decided not to date NCOs. But she had her eye on Hank. He shows up around Fiesta and squires all the girls," Foxy said. "He's delicious to look at and a fun date. But he can be overbearing."

That wouldn't work for long with Foxy.

"Roger and John are taking off this afternoon. We're going to stroll the river," Phyllis said.

Foxy jumped up. "I'll freshen up and meet you in the lobby." She looked at me. "Want to come?"

"Thanks. I have chores to do before I succumb to shopping." I motioned for my check.

"Are you coming to dance rehearsal tonight?" Phyllis asked.

I hesitated. "It might be fun."

"It is. You'll love it." They left.

Maybe I could stay one more night.

My mind raced with images. Monica's murder. A menacing Harry Haddock. I could imagine him being angry enough to kill. The Femmes' boyfriends. Hank Gleason. Dry ice smoke at NIOSA. The skull man with his pin. Too much was going on to worry about my relationship with Sam.

We had a solid plan. He would investigate Harry's background and recent movements and the Femmes' possible connection to drug smuggling. The military would cooperate with SAPD about Hank, Roger and John. Sam would check

John's solar company, and I'd see what he'd learned at his metal plating job. Since Roger was employed by SAWS, I'd try to determine how much he knew about the river.

Twenty-Nine

The San Antonio metal plating company that looked easiest to find was Purely Plating out IH-10 West. Driving north from Loop 410, poor Albatross found himself climbing into the Texas Hill Country. I saw a La Quinta Motor Inn and passed the Dominion, the high-end gated community that was home to corporate executives and some Spurs basketball players.

Texas wildflowers bloomed in open fields, seas of bluebonnets, Indian paintbrush and yellow coreopsis. A sign marked the towns of Leon Springs and Boerne. Before I reached Boerne, I saw the sign for Purely Plating.

I drove up to the facility and faced two long warehouse buildings the size of airplane hangars. A chain-link fence enclosed the front of both buildings and continued around the unmarked building to the right.

The left-hand building had the company name and logo on an awning extending over black glass entry doors. I parked and walked inside. Photographs of luxurious commercial interiors hung on the walls.

The girl behind the desk smiled at me as I entered. "May I help you?"

"My husband and I want to open an upscale restaurant in Houston. We're in San Antonio for Fiesta and heard you create luxury interiors featuring metal trim."

"We do. Would you like to tour our showrooms?"

"That would be great." She paged someone over the intercom. He burst through swinging doors with his hand extended, flashing a salesman's grin.

"I'm Mitch Graves. How can I help you, miss?" He towered over me exuding self-confidence.

"I'm Patricia Wharton. My husband, Stan, and I came from Houston for Fiesta." I told him about our proposed restaurant.

"We do luxury interiors for cruise ships, private aircraft and train cars as well as restaurants. You might get some good ideas. Let me show you."

The first showroom we entered looked like the dining car of a private plane or train. Gold-plated flatware graced the tables. On leather swivel dining chairs, gold-plated accents shone at the end of arm rests. Above a series of small windows, padded upholstered strips flanked a mirrored strip bordered in gold plating that ran the length of the room.

The second room was even larger. He called it a sky view lounge. Windows on outside walls overlooked a series of leather two-seater sofas, each with its own coffee table. Tables, windows, and the faux entrance to another room were lavishly trimmed in gold.

"You do mostly gold plating?"

"We feature gold in the show rooms because it's the most striking. But we plate all kinds of metals with a variety of finishes, whatever the customer wants."

"Can you show me the process?"

"I'm afraid not. The work is done in a separate building because toxic chemicals are used. Our workers wear hazard suits, gloves and masks and follow a stringent set of rules. Plating is done in the adjacent building."

"I see. Can you describe the process?"

"Metals to be plated are placed in a large vat or bath where chemicals clean them of dirt or debris that will prevent the new metal from bonding."

"The chemicals are toxic?"

"Yes. Cyanide compounds effectively remove impurities from metals, but they can be highly toxic mixed with other chemicals. Potassium cyanide, for example, can't be mixed with acids. And the workplace has to be properly ventilated because fumes from various chemicals are dangerous to breathe in."

I wondered what effect they would have if they were dumped into the river.

"Once the metals are cleaned, we use electricity to bond a new metal finish to the source metal. Chromium is a popular metal used in electroplating, but one of the chromium compounds, hexavalent chromium, is highly toxic."

"You must have chemists involved."

"We do. Plus a library of books listing the dangers of mixing certain chemicals and metals. We also make sure wastewater from the bath mixture of metals and chemicals is properly disposed of. Metal plating is an intricate process involving a lot of hazardous materials. Our employees have to be well trained."

"Do you employ people from the military?"

"Sometimes. They're accustomed to following rules."

"We have a friend who used to work in a metal plating plant in San Antonio. Do you happen to know John Abbott?"

"Can't say I do."

"How do you store toxic compounds?"

"They're stored in locked metal cages. Only designated employees can access them. We have stringent rules for removal and handling. Some chemicals look quite innocent. Potassium cyanide, for example, looks like baking soda. We only employ people who know what they're doing. That's why the results are expensive."

He smiled. "We work with designers, get customers'

approval, do the work here and ship the finished product to customers."

"I see. Fascinating. I don't know if we can afford you, but we'll certainly keep you in mind."

"If you sketch your basic idea, we'll present you with a design and price."

I thanked him and left, wondering what training John Abbott received in the Army that prepared him to work in a plating plant. SAPD would have to contact city plating companies to see where he'd worked and exactly what he did.

My next stop was the main office of the San Antonio Water System where Roger Plunkett was employed. I wanted to see if SAWS had any connection to the river.

I drove back to Loop 1604 and veered east toward Highway 281. SAWS main business office was north on 281 North, still in the Hill Country. Spring bluebonnets flourished in the fields.

As San Antonio grew into a region of a million and a half people with thirty-five thousand more expected annually, competing water interests caused City Council to establish a separate utility to deliver water service to the area. The whole region depended on water from the Edwards Underground Aquifer, a geological formation emanating from an underground spring with a recharge zone that covered twelve hundred and fifty square miles. When it rained, the aquifer captured rainwater from the recharge zone. Water was more valuable than gold.

SAWS's responsibility was to protect water resources. I hoped employees were well vetted before they dealt with this treasure, including Roger Plunkett.

I drove up to a building covered with Hill Country limestone, walked in and smiled at the receptionist.

"Hello. We're moving to San Antonio, and I'm interested to learn about restrictions for building over the aquifer. We have a friend who works for SAWS. When we moved from Oklahoma, we lost his contact information. Do you know Roger Plunkett?"

"I'm afraid not."

"Can you help us find how to contact him?"

"We have almost two thousand people working here and in other sub-stations. Human Resources has a complete list of employees."

"Does SAWS hire military veterans?"

"I'm sorry. I don't know. Here's a card for the Human Resources Manager. She's not here now, but you can call for an appointment."

"All right. Thank you."

"Anytime."

I wondered what Sam was learning while I was driving around Texas. I was glad the sun was shining and flowers were blooming.

My next plan was to speak with someone at the San Antonio River Authority. The river was my main concern, and I guessed that SAWS and SARA worked in concert. SARA's office was downtown near the river. From there, it would be an easy drive back to the hotel.

When I located the SARA parking lot, I had to skirt around a couple of trucks outfitted with cranes before I could find a space. I entered the building unsure of what questions to ask, so I picked up a brochure at the information desk.

"Just curious," I said to the smiling girl behind the semi-circular enclosure. I settled into a chair to read.

After devastating floods in 1913 and 1914, the Texas legislature created river authorities to serve regions with river basins. SARA had jurisdiction over 3,658 square miles with all its rivers and tributaries. Headquartered from springs in Olmos Basin and Brackenridge Park, the San Antonio River ran for two hundred and forty miles through counties and towns of landowners, business owners, farmers and ranchers. Then it flowed into San Antonio Bay and into the Gulf of Mexico. SARA had to keep the billion-dollar ecosystem clean, liter free, maintain water quality and protect against floods—a monumental task.

I began to realize poison dumped into the river would dissipate quickly or be detected. The poison would have to be contained, inert and activated at a precise moment.

Watersheds were patrolled and water quality monitored at seven stations throughout the San Antonio River Basin. SAWS and SARA met monthly to share ideas and solutions. Someone who worked at either place could find out where those stations were and when they were monitored. Like Roger Plunkett.

I thanked the receptionist and stepped toward the exit. The trucks with cranes were pulling behind my car as they prepared to leave.

"What are the cranes for?" I asked the girl at the desk.

"They're going to lower barges into the river for the parade tomorrow night. It's fun to watch."

"Where do they go?"

"I'm not sure. It's hard to find."

Thirty

I hopped into Albatross and followed the trucks. They lumbered along and took detours. Streets were closed off so Fiesta parade vehicles and participants could get to the forming area. I was lost. I strained to keep the cranes in sight and followed.

The trucks with cranes finally pulled up behind a similar truck. Its cables and pinchers stretched out from a bridge over the San Antonio River and lowered a flat barge into the water. The barge was about eight by twenty feet long with a small outboard motor in the rear.

I found the nearest parking lot, locked Albatross and ran back to the bridge. A few other onlookers watched the operation. Patrolmen blocked the bridge so no vehicles could drive across. Once a barge floated on the water, a second barge pulled alongside. One assistant pulled the new barge toward him with a grappling hook. A third man jumped onto the new barge, powered up the rear outboard motor and drove the barge under the bridge, where it disappeared. Looking around, I saw nothing but the bridge and ordinary streets. Not far from the bridge, I noticed a concrete circular drive that appeared to coil downwards. No sign marked it. I decided to walk down. No one paid any attention to me as I ambled down the circular drive in a descending curved spiral.

When I reached the bottom, I found myself underneath San

Antonio's streets in an air-conditioned, underground, river-level marina, a huge storage area for river barges. Looking back through the entrance to the river, a narrow passage where the barges entered, I saw no evidence of the curved ramp I'd walked down or the streets I'd stood on. What looked like a barricade on both sides of the entrance looked like it could be activated to close.

I recognized the Yanaguana river boats and walked toward them down a concrete walkway. They were painted red, white and blue with continuous rails behind padded seats, leaving a space where tourists could embark and a smaller gate in the rear where the driver could exit. Toward the back of the boat, a flat-topped driver's stand had a steering wheel behind it and a life-saving ring on the front. Each boat was separated from the next by a concrete pier jutting into the river. Behind me were cages for mechanical repairs—hospital rooms for San Antonio's river barges.

On the other side of the marina, drivers maneuvered newly-retrieved barges into slips. I wondered if these barges would be decorated for the military parade tomorrow night. Walking back on the concrete sidewalk between the Yanaguana boat slips and repair cages, I saw a small elevator ahead and a door marked "Stairs." I entered the elevator and pushed one without any idea where I'd end up. When the door opened, I was in a regular office building. There were a few offices, but the doors had no signs. I walked out the front entrance and turned back to look at the building sign. There was none. A small sign with address numbers stuck up from the grass.

Looking up and down the street, I spotted the bridge where trucks with cranes had been. They were gone. Nothing indicated they'd ever been there. Growing disoriented, I walked toward the bridge, looking for Albatross. I was relieved to spot the parking lot a short distance away. My beloved Wagoneer sat complacently among the others. Gazing back toward the office building, I confirmed it was indeed unmarked. I finally spotted the entrance to the circular ramp I had walked down. Not even an arrow marked the descent.

It appeared no one wanted to advertise the marina's location. Yet I had easily stumbled onto the place where cranes lowered barges into the river. Access to the River Walk Marina was wide open.

I settled into Albatross and called Sam. He said SAPD was checking plating companies to find out where John Abbott used to work.

"I learned at the metal plating company that toxic chemicals are used in the process, but they're locked up," I said.

"That's especially interesting," he said, "because the medical examiner called me after the autopsy to tell me Monica had pulmonary edema, signs of cardiac arrest, and her skin color was reddish, all of which point to cyanide. They found traces of it in her blood, yet Hazmat didn't find traces of cyanide in the room. We're consulting with the San Antonio Testing Laboratory. They can identify poisonous chemicals in various forms, so maybe they'll come up with something. Do they use cyanide in metal plating?"

"He said they use cyanide compounds which could be toxic if mixed with other chemicals."

I knew cyanide compounds were used in low levels in plastics and dyes. Sam said it appeared Monica was putting on makeup in the bathroom. Did someone add chemicals to her makeup so she accidentally combined products that became lethal? I shared my thoughts.

"I guess it's possible," he said. "But I think forensics would have found traces of a substance concentrated enough to kill her. Or somebody else would have been affected by the lethal mixture."

"Like the killer," I said. "How could the killer poison her with cyanide without leaving traces? Or without poisoning himself?"

"I don't know. The ME said he shined fluorescent light on her body looking for bite marks, bruises, bone fragments and substance residue. There were no marks and no residue."

"What did you learn about the hotel roof?"

"Casa Prima has solar panels and skylights on the roof, as do other hotels. Roofers went up there but found nothing out of the ordinary. We checked John Abbott's Sinfully Solar Company and employees. Nobody has a criminal record. A slew of other companies also install solar panels for hotels. They keep records of which hotel panels they check certain days, but they don't log exact times spent on specific roofs. We'll have to keep digging. I did learn something about Monica from the General. She was the ideal enlistee. Her commanding officer recommended she stay in the Army and apply for Officer Candidate School."

"She was quite a girl. What a waste."

"Yes. If you learn anything else or see suspicious activity, let me know."

"I learned about SAWS where Roger Plunkett works. SAWS routinely meets with the San Antonio River Authority. A while back, when the city constructed tunnels to minimize flooding, it created underground storage for river barges. The receptionist at SARA didn't know where barges were stored or how they got them in the river. The brochure from SARA didn't mention it. Yet I found the entrance to the marina. There's no security at all. Anybody could put an item on a boat or carry it with them during a parade. Roger Plunkett undoubtedly knows the location of the marina."

"Good work. Now that we have some facts, we can ask Roger and John the right questions. Did you talk to Grace?"

"No. I didn't have the heart to tell her Monica was definitely pregnant. I was afraid I'd let it slip. And I can't bring myself to tell her she was poisoned."

"I understand."

"The Femmes are having a dance rehearsal tonight for their show at the Arneson Theater. They want me to come."

"And?"

"I might stay one more night." I paused. "Do you think the Femmes are in danger?"

"Why?"

"Because Monica was a Femme and she's dead. And there are other Femmes."

He grew silent.

"What is it?"

"Two Femmes received anonymous notes under their doors, magazine letters pasted on hotel stationery with no fingerprints that read, 'Enjoy your final Fiesta, Femme.' I've put word out to keep an eye on them. Maybe I should come to rehearsal."

"They might be in more danger at the river."

"Why?"

"Well, it's so open. There's so many people there. Anything could happen." I thought about poison dumped in the river and snipers on rooftops but didn't mention it. "The Femmes are here to have fun and seem oblivious to danger. They probably have no idea how to defend themselves."

"I don't think anybody will attack them in the open in front of thousands of people." He stopped to think. "I think it would disrupt Fiesta and cause panic if we tell them to cancel the performance. But it would help if they knew basic protective moves. I'll give them general safety tips after practice. We've been modifying a gadget we've used before. It's a safety mechanism the Femmes could use. We'll get some together. I'll see you at rehearsal."

*   *   *

I'd covered a lot of territory. Traffic was heavy as I snaked my way back toward Casa Prima, doubly worried about the Femmes. Throngs of people milled on the streets, wandering around innocently in their Fiesta finery. I parked in the hotel's underground garage, showed my ID to the officer manning the front door and crossed the lobby to the elevator. Everything looked normal. Most people were eating lunch.

Very few people would be in their rooms, so my timing was good. I had one more thing to do before dance practice.

Thirty-One

I needed to get into the penthouse lounge. I took the elevator to twelve and poked my head out. The hall was deserted. Everybody was either out on the river, eating or napping. Hurrying to the lounge, I looked around again. I knew the regular key to my fifth-floor cubicle wouldn't open the door. I slipped the McVeys' duplicate key into the lock. It clicked open.

Slipping inside, I locked the door trying not to make a sound. If someone attempted to get in, I'd plead ignorance and say I entered to use the bathroom and locked the door to the lounge from habit.

The room was lit only by daylight. Perfect. I could make my way to the bathroom without turning on lights in the main area. Flipping the bathroom light switch, I saw a bathroom twice as large as the one in the McVeys' suite. Casa Prima's thick embroidered taupe towels lay draped over bronzed-gold bars. Floor tiles were covered with the familiar pale brown shag rug, but more floor tiles lay uncovered because of the larger space.

Behind four sinks, bronzed-gold sconces hung between mirrors. Since the ornamental fixtures didn't provide enough light, decorators installed wood soffits covered with beige fabric around the edge of the ceiling to hide subtle light strips. I looked up. Several small recessed light fixtures lay flush with the ceiling, covered by a convex curve of glass held in place by a round metal rim. I looked back at the wall. There was not an adequate number of switches for the lights. I needed to get to those fixtures.

There was no storage closet that might contain a ladder. I didn't remember seeing a ladder in the maid's closet down the hall, but this time of day, I dared not go check. My eyes landed on vanity stools tucked under sinks. I slid one out and positioned it as a step stool to the countertop, kicked off my shoes and stepped onto the counter. It would be easy to reach the fixtures.

There were three recessed light fixtures over two sinks, one over each sink and one between them. I touched the convex cover on the left fixture and tried to twist it. No luck. I poked one end of the cover up and saw the bulb.

Moving to the center fixture, I repeated the action. My hand moved the cover easily, and I saw a larger bulb bright enough to light the sink and the area to the right.

To reach the light over the right-hand sink, I had to step around a footed glass vanity tray beside it on the counter. The tray held tissue, Q-tips, hand lotion and a magnifying mirror with plenty of room left for a woman to place her purse and cosmetics.

I moved under the third fixture, pushed up the cover and peered into an empty space. There was no bulb. This was not a light fixture. There would be sufficient light from other fixtures and light strips on the wall for a person not to notice the absence of light at night. This cover hid a skylight tunnel with more than enough interior rim space to place poison so it could somehow kill a woman below who was making up her face.

Thirty-Two

Rehearsal was in the hotel ballroom. More Femmes came to watch. I needed to tell Sam what I found, even though I'd have to confess to sneaking into the lounge.

The stage was front and center. Staff had moved dining tables to the rear. Electrical outlets for recorded music, microphones and portable amplifiers stood at floor level to the right of the stage. From the back of the ballroom, Femmes pushed two clothing racks full of hanging costumes toward the front. It was hard work weaving unwieldy racks around dining tables.

I went over to the first group of pushers, which included Martha Mayberry. "Here, let me help you."

"Hey, thanks, Aggie. Glad you came."

Costumes hanging on the racks had high-neck bodices with square inserts bordered with white lace trim. Vertical rows of red, blue and yellow ribbons decorated the inserts. Lace trim ran from the shoulders down the middle of elbow-length sleeves. Skirts were huge circles the same colors as the bodices, bright blue or sunflower yellow. The circular skirts were trimmed around the bottom with rows of lace and four-inch wide green, red, and blue ribbon strips that ran in horizontal rows above the hem. I marveled the girls could dance dealing with all that material. A few dark-haired wigs with pigtails hung at the end of the rack.

The dancers went up onstage. Before they ascended the steps, they grabbed long streamers of fabric from a table. They formed two rows with eight women in the front and eight in back. They wrapped the streamers around their waists, then held them out to the sides as far as their arms would reach, spacing themselves on the stage. I thought there would be more dancers, but I realized that two rows of eight women with circular skirts held at arm's length would fill the Arneson Theater stage. Girls with long hair had plaited it into pigtails. The others would have to wear wigs.

Foxy called out from her spot in the center of the back line. "Cindy, will you check the music?"

Cindy put a CD in the player. After a musical introduction, Mexican music poured from the speakers. Cindy adjusted the volume, went back to the beginning and pushed pause.

"Ready girls?" Dancers placed their feet in ballet fifth position, raised their arms to the sides, lifted their chins and smiled. They moved in unison, dancing as if they wore the costumes. By the position of their arms, it was easy to imagine them holding their circular skirts. They might be amateurs, but it would be a fantastic, colorful performance.

Phyllis Morgan, being short, was in the front line. She was flamboyant indeed, putting her whole body into the dance, filled with the rhythm of the music, her moves exaggerated and her smile gleaming. She looked a lot happier without a tower of solar panels on her head. I checked the audience for John Abbott. He grinned like a Cheshire cat. Roger Plunkett smiled beside him.

I looked around. Sam hadn't come to the rehearsal.

I checked the stage for Martha Mayberry. She danced in the back line, all arms and elbows, red hair bouncing to the rhythm. She was as enthusiastic as Phyllis but not as graceful. Girls to her left and right kept an eye on her. When she lifted her arms, with a little extra motion right or left, she might clock them.

Foxy, in the center of the back line, was the tallest girl, even without spiked sandals. She raised her arms stiffly as though she were posing them. Fully into the performance, she looked like Cleopatra holding court.

They danced about fifteen minutes. As soon as they resumed fifth position, onlookers broke into wild applause. I could imagine the roar from the River Walk crowd.

They performed a shorter routine to different Mexican music, a dance calculated to show off the huge circular skirts to greater advantage. As they practiced twice more, my feet began copying their steps. I loved to dance. It was all I could do to sit still.

For the second practice, just as the last song started, a girl in the back line stopped still, put her hand over her mouth and headed for the offstage steps. Looking green, she hustled in front of the stage and raced toward the ballroom exit. We watched, hoping she made it to the nearest bathroom. The dancers dropped their arms and shuffled their feet out of position, chatting among themselves.

"Aggie." I looked up in surprise. Foxy was calling me. "Do you think you can fill in?"

Could I ever. I nodded, hurried for the stage steps, grabbed the length of leftover fabric, took the girl's place in the back row and snapped my feet into fifth position.

I missed a few steps, but overall I was right there with the Femmes. I was having as much fun as anybody. After a couple more practices, sweat beads popped out on a few faces.

"I think we're good," Foxy announced. "Let's call it a day,"

We traipsed down the steps and gravitated to tables, glad to sit. Sam entered the ballroom with a patrolman, walked toward the sound system, picked up the microphone and cleared his throat.

"I'm Detective Sam Vanderhoven, SAPD. I've met some of you. While you're together, I'd like to have your attention for a minute. As you know, a girl was killed in the hotel, an unusual and tragic event. We're working hard to learn how it happened and expect to know very soon who did it so we can put the culprit behind bars. In the meantime, we'd like you to take a few precautions."

I heard intakes of breath. I noticed Sam referred only to what everybody already knew, Monica's death. He didn't mention the call to the mayor or the notes to the Femmes. He had undoubtedly urged the Femmes who received notes to keep silent.

He continued in a voice calculated to soothe. "We have officers at the street and river entrances to the hotel. They're frequently here during Fiesta Week anyway, but they're going to check IDs, so please don't leave the hotel without one. We're going to issue new room keys to everyone in the hotel, so stop by registration for a new key. Your old ones won't work. Your new keys will allow elevators to access your floors and your rooms. If your room is on an upper floor, your new key will also open the penthouse lounge."

Since I had a standard key for my fifth-floor cubicle, his speech wouldn't apply to me. I would destroy the McVeys' key.

"Once you enter your room or the lounge," he said, "close the door behind you. I advise you not to use room service. Use the peepholes in your door and don't open it to anyone."

Girls around me fidgeted nervously.

"We're keeping a protective eye on each of you. I'm having this information delivered to the other Femmes," he said. "Now unless you have questions, we recommend that in case someone accosts you, you learn a few self-defense moves."

The Femmes murmured in worried tones.

He held up his hand. "No need to worry. It's just a

precaution. Does anyone here know self-defense?" He looked at me.

The murmurs grew louder. I timidly raised my hand. "I might be able to help."

They looked at me. I shrugged. "I've learned a little about it."

"All right, Ms. Mundeen. Thank you for volunteering."

It felt more like I'd been conscripted, but I didn't mind helping my friends.

Thirty-Three

The Femmes looked at me and scowled.

"You know self-defense?" Foxy asked.

"I took a few classes." I took a deep breath and motioned them toward me. "So let's gather in a circle and I'll show you some simple moves." While we arranged ourselves, Sam and the officer slipped out of the ballroom. I'd have to tell him later about the solar tunnels and my idea.

"Okay," I said. "In the unlikely event that someone attacks you, you have to fight back." I hoped it was an unlikely event. They looked terrified.

"Remember, you're not trying to hurt somebody. You're trying to injure him so he's ineffective. All you need is force and a target."

They looked doubtful.

"Suppose somebody comes toward you and grabs your arm. With your free hand, shove your palm as hard as you can under his nose or at his Adam's apple. It's called a palm heel strike. He either feels like his nose is broken or he can't breathe. You run.

"Let's say he's closer to you. Don't back up. Step forward, raise your elbow and whack him in the throat with the tip of your elbow or drive it down just below his chest into his solar plexus. It's called an elbow thrust."

Phyllis' eyes expanded to liquid saucers floating in her circular face. Martha's smile was gone. She looked paler by the minute. I hoped these girls were never attacked. It was hard to imagine them as smugglers.

Foxy would probably be my best practice partner to demonstrate the moves. I motioned to her. She strode over, tall and poised. I pantomimed the moves and had her practice.

"Cool," she said. Looking at me dead on, she practiced elbow thrusts with gusto. There was no fear in her face. I made a mental note never to challenge Foxy for position of club officer.

"That's good," I said, "you injure him, then run away screaming." I hoped the girls could injure an attacker *before* they started screaming. They were dancers, not fighters.

I heard a sniffle and pivoted toward Phyllis. She had tears in her eyes.

"I'm too short to poke him in the nose or throat."

"Yes you are, Phyllis. But it's okay. I'm going to teach you defense moves using your legs. It's like dancing. First, the front kick. Plant your feet firmly on the ground. Bend your knee and kick him with a flat foot in the knee or shin. Make sure you're close enough to hit him hard. Don't hesitate. Do it."

I held out my palm, had her kick just short of it over and over and return her foot to the floor until she found the rhythm. "Step, kick. Step, kick."

After the third practice whack, Phyllis' tears disappeared. Her fourth kick was downright aggressive. A big smile spread across her face.

"Good. Good."

The color returned to Martha's cheeks, so I called her over. "We'll practice the round house kick. Twist your body slightly so you can stiffen your leg, swing it around the outside of his leg and hit him about knee level."

She was a natural. I had to watch her closely. With her long legs, if she misgauged, she could break my leg.

"Okay. Good. Now I'm going to teach you the one you've

been waiting for. Bend your knee slightly. Snap your leg straight out so your foot hits right into his groin." Grins appeared. They practiced with gusto.

"They call this one the nut cracker." They practiced over and over, giggling.

They were relaxed and smiling.

"You're a good teacher, Aggie. A good leader."

I never thought I'd hear that from Foxy.

"Thanks. To get good at it," I told them, "you have to repeat these moves in front of the mirror in your room." That brought a round of applause. Kicking was closer to dancing.

I thought they had absorbed all they could. We were finished. Hopefully they would practice. Ideally, they'd never need to use what I taught them. I hoped nothing bad happened to any of them.

They thanked me and filed past the costume rack on their way out, taking their dress and a wig if they needed it.

"Good examples, Aggie."

"We were able to follow what you did."

"Thanks for your help."

Foxy hung back. "You're a good dancer, Aggie. I don't think Sylvia's going to make it. You're about her size. Would you like to dance with us tomorrow night?"

I thought of sitting in the audience at the Arneson, worthless. "You bet I would! Let's keep it quiet though, okay? I'd prefer that Sam and his officers not know."

"Okay. Whatever. Take the dress and wig left on the rack. He'll never recognize you." She grinned, grabbed her costume and sashayed out the door.

I felt hopeful about my friends.

My feet itched. They did that when I expected something to happen.

Thirty-Four

Not wanting to bump into Sam carrying my costume, I made sure the lobby and elevator were clear, rode the elevator to seven and walked down the fire escape stairs to five. Discretion was the better part of valor. I didn't think Sam would want me onstage dancing with the girls. If a problem arose, I could be useful. Plus, I'd have a lot of fun.

I was relieved to find my standard room key still worked. As soon as I got in, I cut up the McVeys' plastic key, wrapped the tiny pieces in newspaper and buried it in the trash.

Then I tried on the costume. The dress fit, and the wig rendered me unrecognizable. Perfect. How could I resist this opportunity? I was going to participate in Fiesta! I hung them in my mini-closet and considered calling Sam. I'd describe the tunnel skylights, explain how one would have been above Monica's head where she put on makeup, and confess I had decided to dance.

He would try to talk me out of it, of course. He was already under terrific pressure to solve this crime. We would quarrel.

My phone rang. It was Sam.

"How did self-defense go?"

"I think the girls got it, but I hope they don't have to use the moves. I don't know if they'll practice. Have you learned more since this afternoon?"

"We verified Roger Plunkett has access to information

about the river. John Abbott was not cleared by the military to access chemicals at plating companies or anywhere else. That would require special training. But he has installed skylights. SAPD questioned your friends about drugs but later found evidence implicating suspects who are now in jail awaiting trial. They think they're the right guys, but they can't conclusively exonerate your friends."

"Then I guess I better tell you what I learned researching Martha Mayberry. She worked in gift shops in Laredo and Nuevo Laredo and at River Center and North Star Mall, moving from shop to shop. She was never changed with a crime. Foxy married three times. It appeared she received a substantial portion of her husband's assets from each divorce, because she never worked. Nobody ever filed charges against her."

"My lawyer friend said Howard Strong sued her when they divorced and kept most of his assets."

"And she still has no record of employment?"

"No. She could have found an easier way to make money."

"Drugs."

"Yes," he said. "I guess we're back into watch-and-wait mode."

"I guess so." I decided not to tell him I was dancing with the Femmes.

"Aggie?"

"Yes?"

"Don't forget to be careful."

It was late. I was too tired to go downstairs to eat, so I decided to bathe, wash my hair and check my email. I wrapped my head in a towel and powered up the laptop. Grace had forwarded me a letter addressed to Dear Aggie.

Dear Aggie,

I've been married twice and it didn't work out. Relationships with men are so complicated. The only constant in my life has been my girlfriends. They've stayed with me through highs and lows. Sometimes we irritate one another but remain friends. I wish I could find a man to marry who would be my best friend, a man I can trust, who cherishes me, who always has my back. Have you ever wished for that? Maybe you already have it. If you do, tell me how to find it. For me, it never seems to work that way.

Hopeful but hapless,
Harriet

Dear Harriet,

I doubt that you're hapless. Sometimes we're just lucky. Circumstances are right for us to meet the man that's right for us. Sometimes, we're unlucky. We're so eager to love and be loved, we're apt to fall for superficialities. Then we discover it's the wrong man. Has that happened to you?

Here's what I recommend: learn to be kind, faithful, and grow in your potential. Be content with who you are. Don't manufacture traits for a man because you think he's attractive. It might be wishful thinking. Work on being the best person you can be. When you meet the right man, he'll see the good in you. You will have grown wise enough to recognize the good in him. Don't be too eager or in a hurry. Good marriages last a lifetime. And love lasts forever.

Meanwhile, cherish your girlfriends. They are jewels in your crown.

Sometimes hapless, always hopeful,
Aggie

I was completely honest with Harriet and was, naturally, thinking about Sam. I knew he could be my best friend and would always have my back. He just wasn't crazy about being put in a position of having to protect me. If I expected him to trust me, I had to learn to be honest with him.

Complete honesty was hard for me. I thought about the costume and wig in the closet. I was still working on the trust issue. Maybe because of Lascivious Lester. Oh, well. A Fiesta dance was a small thing. I didn't intend to do anything dangerous. I simply wanted to be able to help my friends and have some fun.

I shut down the laptop and lay awake thinking about how a killer could poison Monica with cyanide without leaving a trace.

Thirty-Five

The girls and I had agreed to meet in the hotel restaurant for a late brunch. We thought it should be the last time we ate before we gathered at Arneson Theater at six to prepare for the performance. We were excited and dancing took energy. We didn't want to be full of food and wanted to get to the theater before crowds gathered. We would see what was backstage, decide the best way to make our entrance, position ourselves onstage and test the music.

When I reached the dining room, they had finished eating.

"We wondered if you were coming. We waited as long as we could," Martha said.

"I had a hard time getting up this morning."

"I was afraid you might have Sylvia's bug," Foxy said. "She's been in her room since rehearsal. I think she's down for the count." She looked at her watch. "It's almost one o'clock. I guess we might as well go to our rooms and rest before we start dressing for the performance."

I hoped these women weren't drug runners. I liked them. We were walking toward the exit when Sam appeared at the door with two uniformed officers.

"I'm afraid there's been an emergency in the hotel." We froze. He held up his hands. "It's nothing to endanger you, but we'd like you to please remain in the restaurant and not leave the hotel until we sort it out. These officers will assist you. Ms. Mundeen, please come with me."

Something terrible had happened. I hoped it didn't have anything to do with my sneaking into the lounge.

He led me to the lobby.

"What is it?"

"There's been another murder. It's someone you know, so you don't need to see her."

Who could it be? I'd just seen the Femmes. Surely Grace wouldn't come looking for me at the hotel. "It's not Grace, is it?"

"No."

"Or the Femmes?"

"No."

"In a suite?"

"Yes."

I swallowed. "All right, then I'd like to see the victim. If it's someone I know, I can verify their identity. Plus I might see something in the room to trigger my memory and help you solve the crime."

He leaned forward, hair flopping on his forehead. "I think we can solve this without you."

"I know you can. But I'm too involved to be excluded."

"I don't know why you want to see this." He swiped his chin with the back of his hand and studied me. "Aggie"—he put up a finger like he was about to scold me—"use the elevator to a floor near the top, take the stairs to the penthouse and slip into the hall so nobody sees you. Act like you were up there to see the penthouse and had no idea about the crime. It's absolutely against SAPD rules for you to be involved with this. Go straight to the crime scene before anyone can stop you. If somebody does stop you, I'll say I allowed you up because you're working on getting your PI license. Once you identify the victim, you should leave. We may have a serial killer here. Someone bent on causing havoc during Fiesta. The hotel is going to be in a state of semi-lockdown. Anyone entering or leaving will be given a thorough check. I can vouch for you now, and SAPD will let you leave. You shouldn't be here, Aggie. It's dangerous. This is the best time for you to go home."

"You'll be here."

"I have to stay and help solve this, Aggie. You know that. We're dealing with a maniac. He may not be through killing. Otherwise, why would he kill now? During Fiesta Week? These killings could be a prelude to something larger. I have to stay. And you need to go."

"I understand." I took a deep breath. "Okay. I'm ready to see the victim."

He took the elevator. I did as instructed, took stairs to the penthouse and followed him and the officers down the hall from a distance. He stopped at a room with yellow crime scene tape. I steeled myself and rushed up to peer inside. The room was identical to the others, the scene horribly familiar. Lying on the beautiful sofa, one arm draped over the back of a silk pillow and one hanging to the floor, was Sara Giles. Former wife. Current maid. My new friend.

I covered my mouth and turned away. "I know her. It's Sara Giles, the maid who found Monica. Poor girl." I started to cry.

"I'm sorry. You shouldn't have come up here. I'll escort you to the elevator." He told the patrolmen I had mistakenly come up and was going to leave the floor.

Just as my door closed, Rick Montaya emerged from the other elevator with more patrol officers. I sat in the lobby and waited for Sam. He finally came down to the lobby, drew up a chair and spoke softly. Authorities from the sheriff's office, military police and National Guard were on their way since they routinely assisted with Fiesta Week. He needed to check everything about the scene before talking with officers from other agencies.

"We're going to meet authorities in the penthouse lounge.

We've started doing background checks on everybody leaving or entering," he said, studying my face. I tried to relax my jaw.

Valerie Garrett walked up looking sympathetic.

"Why don't you and Valerie go to the restaurant?" he said. "Hotel guests and staff are there. SAPD and sheriff's deputies are talking with everybody to maintain calm. Valerie, you come back up in a few minutes."

I frowned. Sam returned to the elevator. Valerie walked me to another part of the lobby. We sat while she attempted to comfort me and ask me questions. I sniffled and didn't answer. I think she meant well, but I didn't feel like talking. When I did, I'd tell Sam whatever I had to say.

When she emphasized that I should leave, heat rose up my back. My spine stiffened. I wasn't about to leave Sam. Not with voluminous, voluptuous Valerie. And a killer on the loose.

She took my elbow, stood me up and suggested we go to the restaurant.

I went with her and thanked her for her concern. When she went to talk to other officers, I went to sit with the Femmes and whispered to them that Sara was dead. There were gasps, then silence. We were in shock.

"I wish I hadn't said those things about Sara," Foxy said.

After about an hour, Sam appeared at the restaurant and announced that the Fabulous Femmes should go to the ballroom for a quick practice. They looked at each other quizzically.

As each girl left the restaurant and passed by Sam, he gave them his most reassuring smile. I went last and stopped to face him.

"I'm going to the ballroom with the Femmes," I said. "And I'm not leaving."

"I didn't think you would."

Thirty-Six

When the Femmes and I entered the ballroom, SAPD officers, military police, sheriff's deputies and National Guard officers stood against the walls. Harry Haddock stood among them, fidgeting with his hands.

Sam walked to the stage and turned on the microphone. "I regret to tell you that another woman has been murdered in this hotel."

Faces blanched. He didn't give Sara's name or identify her as a former Femme. There was no sense frightening everybody.

"We're here to apprehend this killer and protect you. We want you to continue your plans to perform at Arneson Theater. We'll have tight security there and here at the hotel. We want citizens to continue to enjoy Fiesta, and we think we have a better chance to catch this criminal if events proceed as usual. We're taking extra precautions."

Another officer stepped forward. "Since last night's rehearsal, we've adapted devices to protect you with additional security. We had a few transmitters made for some of you to pin to the neck of your costumes. As you can see," he held up one of the pins, "they look like various Fiesta medals. A small transmitter is secured between the medal and the pin that attaches to your clothes. You reach under the medal to turn it on and off. It looks like you're just fingering the pin. Each device has two frequencies. If an officer pushes one button, you'll hear him talking through the transmitter. To talk to the officer, you push the other button. Just turn your head slightly, smile and speak normally above the pin. Twist the buttons to adjust the volume. You're in touch with a law officer at all times. If you see or hear anything suspicious, report it at once, give your name, location and the location of the suspicious event. We radio it to other officers. Leave the device on listening mode and you won't be heard. If you feel confident you can use the device to contact us, come up and we'll show you how to activate it."

Foxy was first in line.

"Psst, Phyllis," I said. "Get me one." I couldn't get it myself because Sam didn't know I was dancing with the Femmes. Phyllis nodded and followed Foxy. Two women I hadn't met stepped in behind her. They must have received the anonymous letters, and SAPD told them to line up for the gadgets.

"Pin the device high," the officer said, "next to your collar bone."

I moved close enough to see how the gadget worked. "If you're wearing it now, leave it on," the officer said. "If you're wearing other medals, move them around to look natural and continue to wear them. We'd like you to get used to the gadgets and return to the restaurant. We believe the victims were poisoned, so don't ingest anything except food and drink from the hotel dining room. Room service is cancelled. All edible items are in the restaurant. Wait there until time to dress for your performance. An officer will accompany each of you to your rooms, check them out and wait outside for you to dress. When everyone is costumed and back in the restaurant, you'll meet riverside by the hotel, and officers will escort you to the theater."

I waited until the others filed out, went to Sam and whispered, "You didn't reveal everything about security, did you?"

"No. We'll have armed police at Arneson Theater when the

girls perform. But we need a spotter in the crowd—someone sitting in Arneson Theater seats about a third of the way up from River Walk level who knows the whole layout—the stage, theater seats, entrance to La Villita, the girls and how the performance goes. Do you think you could be the spotter and communicate with us if you see something unusual? You'll be able to see everything from there and you'll wear this pin with the communication device." He handed it to me. "You shouldn't be in danger with police stationed all around. I'll be there too, but you probably won't see me. There's always some risk, but I think it's minimal. What do you think?"

"What about the girls? They're my friends. How can I help them onstage if I'm sitting across the river?"

"We'll have armed police backstage."

"You want me to just sit in the audience like a tourist and wait to see what happens?"

"That's basically what we're all doing. You're more likely to recognize something unusual."

I was flattered he asked me to help, and I was trying to be agreeable. I told him I thought poison could have been placed inside the skylights and I still thought somebody could devise a way to poison the river. He didn't seem impressed.

How could I promise to sit in the audience like a bump on a log?

"Time is running out," he said. "You have the pin. We need to set up surveillance."

Actually, I had two pins.

"You'd better get an officer to accompany you upstairs and check your room."

Thirty-Seven

Sam was bullheaded. He wasn't listening to me. He didn't trust me to make decisions. Trust was a two-way street.

Scanning the room, I saw a young officer and headed for him.

"Hi. I'm Aggie Mundeen, a friend of Detective Sam Vanderhoven. I understand we're supposed to ask an officer to walk us to our rooms."

"Yes, ma'am. I'm Bobby Fleming. I'll be happy to help you." I had fallen in love with Texas courtesy.

On the elevator, I said, "I'm sorry you're having to deal with this. I imagine you'd much rather be partying at Fiesta."

He grinned. "Rookie officers do what we're told." We talked about upcoming Fiesta events. When we got to five, I opened my cubbyhole with the key.

"It's tiny. Shouldn't take you long to look."

With his hand on his holster, he looked around the room, under the bed and into the bathroom and closet. If he noticed the costume, he didn't comment. He either assumed I was performing with the ladies or had some weird Fiesta get-up ready for action.

"Looks clear, ma'am."

"Good. It won't take me long to dress while you wait outside."

I freshened up, donned the costume, attached the

transmitter pin Phyllis gave me to the bodice and hid the one Sam gave me in my waistband. As I stuffed my hair under the pigtail wig, I considered what I could say to Officer Bobby Fleming to make him leave his post.

I called through the door. "I forgot. I have important information about the murders for Detective Sam that I neglected to give him. He's so busy, I don't want to interrupt him with a call. I'm half dressed. If I slip you a note under the door, will you take it to him?"

"I don't know…"

"It's critical to the case. He needs it ASAP. He'll be very glad you brought it to him, Bobby. He'll be impressed. If you hurry, you can catch him in the lobby."

That was the last place Sam would be. I scribbled some lines on a sheet of paper in case Bobby read the note: "Confirmed information about X and Y but could not determine location of T." I folded it twice, wrote "DET. V" on the outside and slipped it under the door.

Bobby retrieved the note. "I'll be right back." I heard him sprint toward the elevator.

I did a final check on the strange woman looking at me from the mirror, stuffed the flip-phone down my bra and peeked into the hall. The corridor was clear. I headed for the fire exit and was barreling down the stairs when my phone rang. It was Sam. I stopped on a landing to dig out the phone.

Before I could speak, he started talking. "The ME said cyanide victims usually ingest the poison. But the testing lab says potassium cyanide looks like white crystalline powder. It can be activated with acidic liquid to turn into hydrogen cyanide gas. That's what he thinks killed the women."

"That's horrible," I puffed.

"You sound out of breath."

"Rushing to get dressed. Gas could come through the

skylight," I said. I clamored down the steps, covering my phone to hide the echo of my clattering feet.

"Or from nasal spray," he said. "Or from an inhaler from a hospital or pharmacy. But spray would dissipate in the air."

"Or up through the roof." I said. "I guess anybody could get a sprayer."

"Right. We learned more about Hank Gleason. Before he was in the Army, he left a pregnant bride at the altar. He married another woman, and she divorced him. When he learned his third wife was pregnant, he left her, but they're not legally divorced. He pays her a bundle."

I couldn't blame Monica for falling for those purple-blue eyes. "If he got Monica pregnant, he'd be in a fix, still married to another woman and not willing to marry Monica. If she told the Army, it could end his career. We're back to the same circle of people who touched Monica," I said. "Except Sara wasn't really part of the group."

"We need answers," he said, "and we're running out of time." He hung up.

I reached the first floor and peered across the lobby. Sam wasn't in sight.

The Femmes were streaming out of the hotel entrance to the river. If I hurried I could blend with the group and try to protect them. I caught up, slipped into line behind Phyllis, pulled the transmitter pin Sam gave me from my waistband and pressed it into her palm. "It's an extra," I said. "Give it to somebody who didn't get one."

By the time Sam got my scribbled message and realized I'd slipped away from the sweet young officer, I'd be where I needed to be. I felt guilty not following his orders. I shouldn't make it difficult for him to protect me. He hated that. And I'd probably be safer sitting in the theater seats with SAPD knowing where I was.

But I just couldn't sit there knowing my friends were in danger on the other side of the river. Armed police officers backstage would help, but these killers were cunning. I was afraid they might do something that looked innocuous, and nobody would realize it was lethal until it was too late. If I was near my friends, I'd be better positioned to realize what was happening and help.

I knew Sam was too concerned about my safety to let me dance with the Femmes. And too bullheaded to seriously consider poison gas coming through the skylight.

We Femmes walked along the river in a line with one police officer in front and two in the rear. We caused a stir in our costumes. Tourists looked at us and smiled, oblivious to the fact we were escorted by SAPD. We strolled along one side of the river until we crossed over Rosita's Bridge to reach the side with the Arneson stage. We descended the bridge to river level and looked up at the stage where we'd perform.

"It's smaller than I thought," Martha said. The flooring was made of wood strips that looked like they'd been sealed but not stained. The stage curved outward toward the river.

Stucco buildings to the left of the stage probably held dressing rooms. There were plugs outside on the stucco walls where Cindy could plug in her sound equipment. Dark heavy wood doors, deeply recessed into the stucco, apparently led to dressing rooms. After officers opened the doors and checked the rooms, we entered and looked around. One of the rooms had a toilet stall, which was good. We had an hour to wait before we performed. Steps between the two dressing rooms led outside to the back of the building. The officers scoured the area. One took a position near the back steps, and the other stood just inside the heavy riverside doors.

"Let's go onstage," Foxy said. "Back line first and front line second. To make onlookers curious, we'll hold out our skirts and smile while we space ourselves. Once we get our spacing right, Cindy can turn on the music. We won't dance. We'll just swish our skirts. When the music ends, we can exit back into the hall toward the dressing rooms and wait there until show time."

I was in the back row, far right, as viewed from across the river. With taller girls in the center, we sloped down toward the ends. I lead my row onstage with the breeze rippling my skirt. I felt very much part of Fiesta. With our arms fully stretched, holding our skirts, we spaced ourselves so front line girls could spread their skirts without blocking the view to anyone behind.

Cindy started the music. We swished in place. I had a chance to study what was happening across the river. People dribbling in from La Villita filled the top rows of Arneson theater seats. People coming from the River Walk settled into lower seats. The raspa man came by rolling his cart selling cups of shaved ice with different flavors of sugary colored syrup poured over it. It occurred to me one of the colored syrups could contain poison.

Children in the audience wore circular headbands that blinked lights. Some waved lighted wands. I envied their happy innocence.

Men with short haircuts wearing guayaberas covered with medals stood at intervals around the periphery of the seating area. They were obviously cops. The long shirts were perfect for hiding holsters. I didn't see Sam. As dusk settled on the river, tree lights started twinkling.

When our music stopped, people applauded. As we traipsed offstage, we heard sighs of disappointment.

Cindy, also in costume, stood and picked up the microphone next to her CD player. "That's just a taste of the delightful show to come. In a few more minutes, you'll see the Fabulous Femmes dancing to your favorite Mexican music!"

For an amateur group, the Femmes were quite professional.

It seemed like an eternity passed before Foxy gave the go ahead. "Okay, girls! Get your smiles on, swish your skirts and parade out onstage to take your positions." Cindy played the music louder. We took our places to wild applause. Theater seats at every level were filled with people crowded together.

As we smiled in place, Cindy played our musical introduction. We listened intently. When the main number started, we broke into action. I was nervous and somewhat out of step, but the number went well with no serious mishaps. People clapped and yelled.

When our dance number ended, we grew still again, smiling with our skirts held out and our feet in fifth position. Cindy started the music to our second number and we burst into dance. It was easier now. We were into it.

Thirty-Eight

When our dances were over, everybody shouted and applauded. We swished and smiled. Too bad we didn't have a few more numbers. I hated to leave the stage.

Foxy told the girls in the front line to sit down, stage front, and space themselves at equal intervals. They dangled their feet over shrubs planted riverside and spread their skirts. From the spectator side, they would look like dolls peeping out above fabric draped across the front of the stage. I knew which girls had transmitter pins.

Stage right, a barge pulled up for the rest of us. We went down four steps to river level and stepped onto the barge, waving and smiling to the crowd. The barge glided across the river and deposited us on the opposite bank. Foxy had given us the same instructions: sit at river's edge and spread your skirts. Onlookers cheered as we extended our skirts between us on the flagstones. I ended up on the far right of the audience, facing the stage. Phyllis sat about eight feet to my left, close enough to talk. I fingered my transmitter and heard Sam's voice. He probably didn't know for sure it was me. I inadvertently cleared my throat.

"Where are you, Aggie? That was cute the way you managed to ditch my officer at the hotel." I turned down the volume. "Don't you ever do what I ask? Nobody has a clue where you are. Are you one of those girls by the river in those stupid wigs?

Without any protection? Do you want to get yourself killed? I should've known better than to trust you."

His last words hurt me. I should have told him I wanted to dance with the girls instead of scouting from the audience. He wouldn't have liked it, but he might have agreed. Actually, I doubted it.

My vantage point here was perfect. I didn't need to turn my head much to see every row of theater seats, the whole stage and both ways down the river. If I didn't learn to deal with this trust issue, though, I was going to lose Sam. I didn't blame him for being furious. I just couldn't take his tirade right now. I pushed the button and turned him off.

I turned toward Phyllis. "I might have just lost the only man I've ever loved."

"Oh, Aggie. I know what you mean. I might be losing John too. He used to be so loving. Lately, he gets moody and shuts me out. And Martha says Roger is starting to drink a lot."

Music coming from a float drifted toward us. I looked left up the river, then glanced up into the crowd to check for suspicious behavior. Everything looked normal. I turned my attention back to the river.

Fingering the pin, I turned it on to see if Sam was still there. He must have heard a click.

"I finally got us a suite, by the way. Too bad you're not interested in sharing it." He thought he was talking to me, but with the transmitters switched, he could have been propositioning somebody else.

I clicked off the transmitter. I didn't want to be found. I doubted he could locate me if my device wasn't turned on.

Music from the float grew louder as it rounded the bend. Huge paper flowers in fuchsia, sunflower yellow, orange and purple, Fiesta colors, encircled the low fence around the barge.

The craft floated slowly toward the front of the Arneson

Theater. "The Yellow Rose of Texas" blared through the air. City dignitaries stood on the float and waved: San Antonio's Mayor, Chief of Police, Fire Chief, City Council members and Bexar County Commissioners. Weighted with so many people, the float rode low in the water. The boat driver, wearing a colorful guayabera with Fiesta medals and a panama hat, stood proudly near the back of the craft behind the steering column and guided the barge. Like everyone else, I waved and clapped. Knowing a crazy person had called the mayor, I stared at each person on the barge. Somewhere in the Arneson seats behind me, Sam was holding his breath.

As the float passed beyond me, I did a quick perusal of the stands. People in the audience sat back down. Nothing looked suspicious or out of the ordinary.

As the second float appeared around the bend, "The Star-Spangled Banner" filled the air. Handsome men and women in dress uniforms representing the military services stood around the float and saluted the crowd. Pillows in Fiesta colors lay inside the barge rail. Tall heavy vases of shining hammered Mexican silver anchored the corners and glittered off soldiers' medals.

Outside the low rail, vivid paper flowers fluttered in the breeze. Flags from every military branch, with the American flag attached in the center, flew behind the barge.

General Dayton, Ft. Sam Houston's Commander, stood in front of the panama-hatted driver. What a coup for the man who had the honor of steering the barge honoring the military. Filed with pride, my hand over my heart, I watched the fine soldiers who protected us.

As the barge passed in front of me, the barge slowed and the soldiers stood at ease. Ironically, the barge driver wore more medals than the officers. I squinted and leaned forward. Was it Roger? The driver's hat shadowed his face. His medals were not pinned in precise rows. They were randomly skewed. He reached to tap the General's shoulder with a tanned arm and pointed to a glass sitting on top of the driver's stand. When the General nodded, he picked up the glass and poured liquid from his own water bottle into the General's glass, simultaneously drawing a mask from under the front of his panama hat down over his nose.

The General was about to be poisoned. I clicked on the transmitter and yelled. "It's him, Sam. He's making poison in that glass. We have to stop him before he can do it. It's the killer! Stop the barge!"

The driver nudged the General toward the driver's gate where he would shove him into the water with his poisoned cocktail.

Sam charged down the Arneson steps toward the river. I knew he would leap into the river to get the killer. I thought I could get to the barge first.

Thirty-Nine

"I'm going in!" I shouted so loud, four rows of onlookers jumped. Femmes looked shell-shocked.

Foxy screamed, "Aggie sees the killer. Stop the barge. Follow her!"

I tripped on my skirt and felt flat on my face in the river.

I came up and fought my way through shallow water, yelling at the soldiers. "The driver is trying to poison the General. Stop him!"

Girls on the stage jumped in, skirts ballooning. Wigs airborne. Girls on the bank rolled in, their skirts dragging behind them. Their wigs came off and floated on the surface like algae.

Soldiers leaped toward the duo. They grabbed the General and knocked him away from the driver. One soldier grabbed the culprit's water bottle and the General's glass, retreated from the melee and held the containers upright as the barge rocked under them. Two others tackled the driver and dragged him down. Another soldier cut off the motor. Femmes clung to the boat like barnacles, colorful fabric floating behind them like soggy flags.

"Drag the barge to the bank," I gurgled.

Grasping the barge with one hand, wrestling our skirts with the other, our wigs floating in the water, we inched the barge toward the bank.

When the barge neared the bank, Sam grabbed it and

pulled it toward him, dragging us with it. He leaped onto the barge and cuffed the culprit.

SAPD officers rushed to stabilize the barge. We turned loose and slogged our way to places on the bank to get out. It was slow going. With waterlogged skirts, we looked like multi-colored slugs.

We struggled, helping each other drag skirts onto the river bank. People near the steps came to help. I looked up into a set of purple-blue eyes. Hank Gleason grinned down and sized me up, a wigless, plastered-haired creature.

"I didn't think we'd meet again like this," he said.

I wished I were back in the river ducking under the water.

Foxy, her skirt more in the river than out, dripped and ogled Hank. She smiled and started to speak but lost her footing. Twirling her arms like windmills, she splashed back into the water.

"Nice to see you, Hank," I said. "We'll get her out." One was always cordial in Texas.

Soldiers hauled the driver off the boat. With his hat off, wet hair plastered to his sorry skull, John Abbott looked like the rat he was.

Sam and SAPD surrounded him and marched him up the steps to La Villita toward the street where the police van waited.

The Hazmat team arrived and went to the spot on the barge where the military officer held the glass and bottle upright. "Thank you, officer. We'll take over and secure them for transport."

Another Hazmat officer shouted through his megaphone, "Please clear the area." Once SAPD evacuated the theater, the Hazmat team carried secured receptacles up the steps, through La Villita and out to their waiting van.

Sam stood under the arch to La Villita with a megaphone, yelling in clipped syllables. "All members of the Femmes dancing group meet in the hotel ballroom as soon as you get on dry clothes." He looked straight at me. "*Now.* Officers will check your rooms. There will be an all-points bulletin issued for Femmes who are not in the ballroom in fifteen minutes."

I doubted he'd put out APBs on a bunch of dripping women. But I knew better than to disobey his orders. I'd never seen him so angry.

Well, maybe a couple of times.

I dragged my bedraggled body up the steps, careful not to look him in the eye. I'd never see the inside of that penthouse suite. The meeting in the ballroom might be the last time I'd ever see Sam.

Forty

Femmes sat at tables in the ballroom, exhausted, shocked and mostly dry. Few wore makeup. Our hair either dripped or had dried in strange configurations. Nobody looked like a Madhatter, Flamboyant or Foxy. We resembled drowned rodents.

Phyllis Morgan's eyes were red. Tears dribbled down her face. "I can't believe John could actually kill somebody."

Foxy, Martha and I patted her hand.

"Did he kill both our members?" she sniffed.

"It looks like he did," I said. "Did Monica dump him for an officer?"

Phyllis nodded, tears streaming down her cheeks. "I didn't want to tell about that and get him in trouble. She dumped him not long after he was discharged from the service. I guess her rejection was one blow too many."

Thank goodness being rejected by Lester the Louse didn't have the same effect on me. It had an effect, though. I had trouble trusting anybody. I was beginning to realize that my headstrong actions made it difficult for people to trust me.

"Why would he kill poor Sara?" Foxy asked.

"Sara told me she saw two men enter and leave Monica's room," I said. "Maybe one of them was John, and he knew Sara saw him. She didn't know who they were, but John probably thought she could identify him."

Martha groaned. "I hope the other man wasn't Roger."

SAPD and military officers stood guard around the room. Sam strode to the microphone. "You ladies were very brave today. But what you did was foolish. The man you went after is a killer. He confessed to killing two of your friends in this hotel."

Phyllis closed her eyes.

Sam continued. "He intended to kill the General and anybody near him with hydrogen cyanide gas he created by pouring acidic liquid into that glass with potassium cyanide crystals concealed under a penetrable insert. He was going to shove it under the General's nose, then push him and the glass into the river. The results could have been catastrophic. You ladies, jumping in the river toward him like you did, could have been the first casualties." His gaze flipped to me. He squeezed his eyes shut and shook his head.

I thought the gas would have dissipated before it hit the river.

"Hazmat is checking public areas of the hotel for poison, including the swimming pool. Military teams are helping expedite the process. They don't expect to find anything and will advise us when it's safe to return. You have to stay out of your rooms while they check for poison. They've already checked the restrooms here in the ballroom in case you need to use them while you wait."

"This is one convention we'll never forget," Foxy said. "I wonder if they'll dredge the river for wigs."

When the girls rose, chairs scraped the floor. I got up with the pack and scurried toward the ladies' room. The last thing I wanted was to face Sam. He'd be furious despite the fact that I realized what the killer was doing, and the girls and I stopped him. Plus the soldiers, of course.

If I hadn't ditched the young police officer planted outside my room, I could never have gotten onstage, much less to the river bank.

"How could I be attracted to someone so evil?" Phyllis sobbed, padding to the bathroom.

I put my arm around her. "We're all subject to it," I said. "We just want to be loved. We're charmed into *thinking* we're in love. The more charming a guy is, the more he can blind us to what he's really like." Hank Gleason's megawatt smile and purple-blue eyes flashed before me. I wondered how many hearts he'd broken.

Phyllis sniffed. "John could really be charming."

Waiting for stalls, the girls discussed how to be more discerning. They contemplated going to the bar once Hazmat cleared it. They could discuss the matter, listen to music and cheer themselves up.

"I think I'll go to my room," I said.

I wanted to be alone. I needed time to think.

Forty-One

In my room, I powered up the laptop. Sure enough, Grace sent me a letter for Dear Aggie.

Dear Aggie,

I've been independent as long as I can remember. My father was in the Air Force, so our family moved around a lot. I attended twelve different schools. As an only child, I conversed more with adults than with kids my own age. Every time I'd try to make friends, it was time to move. I found it easy to meet people, but I was afraid to form close friendships because I knew they couldn't last.

I've met a man I'm crazy about who comes from a big, close-knit family. He seems intrigued by my independence, but it's starting to come between us. I'm a freelance photographer. Magazines seek me out and send me on assignment. I go where my imagination leads me. I love what I do. When I take off on a quest, my boyfriend thinks I should consult him first. He's an engineer with a nine to five job, so he couldn't go with me anyway. I stay in touch, so he knows I'm safe, but he's started asking me details of where I've been and what I did. I love this man and don't want him to reject me, but he's starting to bug me. I don't want to change who I am. I've never been on a leash and don't intend to start now. I'm starting to wonder if it's possible to be independent and be committed to another person. What do you think?

Going Buggy in Baton Rouge

Buggy struck a nerve. Answering her would require extra consideration. If I sat by the pool, maybe I could clear my head.

The pool area was deserted. After two murders and another one attempted at the river, nobody was inclined to swim. It was growing dark around the pool except for lights shining in from the hotel. The pool itself was lighted from within, a shimmering oasis. From flower beds, light beams shone up on tree trunks. I found a chaise in semi-darkness where I could be nearly invisible but could see to write on my notepad.

Relationships I witnessed tumbled across my brain: Monica's determination to date only officers, which led her to reject John Abbott. Piled on top of his general discharge, Monica's rebuff prompted him to kill her and Sara and try to murder General Dayton. He wanted revenge on the women and the military he thought rebuffed him.

John was fueled by revenge. I just wanted to survive rejection and find redemption and love. Lester definitely damaged my self-esteem. Instead of killing somebody, I decided to reclaim my confidence and self-worth. Perhaps that explained my eagerness to forge ahead, no matter what.

I wanted to be friends with Foxy, Phyllis, and Martha. Yet I was quick to suspect they were involved in a crime. I couldn't believe they were so devious, but I couldn't prove they were innocent. I was glad they never knew I checked on them. How could they be my friends knowing I didn't trust them?

It was time to call my dear friend, Grace. She picked up on the second ring.

"Hello?"

"You sound better, Grace."

"I am better. You must know who killed Monica. Tell me."

"John Abbot, a man she dated. His Army service wasn't up to par and he received a general discharge. It was a devastating blow. When Monica told him she decided to date only officers, he went off the deep end and killed her."

"That's horrible. Just for that. Imagine."

"Yes. He did it with a gas that killed her instantly in the bathroom of her hotel suite. I want you to know she didn't suffer." I didn't know how true that was, but I wanted it to be Grace's truth. I decided not to tell her about Sara. "He tried to kill Ft. Sam Houston's Commanding General with the same gas on a parade float today."

"Unbelievable. In front of thousands of people? He must be mentally ill."

"I think so. Police arrested him, he's in custody, and the General is safe."

"Thank God for that."

"How are you doing?" I heard Boffo barking.

"It's been an interesting couple of days. I contacted the California film company where Michael worked. I thought I should tell him about Monica. He might want to help plan her funeral. They referred me to an Austin film company that hired him, and I called him. He loves the new company and thinks he'll be there permanently. With his new bride, Claire, he drove down yesterday to see me. He met her in Austin, it was love at first sight, and they married about six months ago. I adore them both. We're all planning Monica's funeral together. Even Boffo accepted them."

It was great to hear her laugh.

"His company plans to do a film set on the River Walk, so he'll be here often. They're expecting their first child."

"What wonderful news. Part of your family is back."

"Yes. It seems we all needed a family and we found one. They're having a girl. They've decided to name her Grace."

I was thrilled for my dear friend. I closed my eyes, thankful that Grace's heart was on the mend.

My relationship with Sam had taken a major hit. I sympathized with Buggy in Baton Rouge. During this ordeal, I started to feel controlled. Sam said he had to stay in the hotel, but he told me to leave. He told me to go to the hotel restaurant with Valerie but told her to come back upstairs. After Sara was killed, he told me to leave again.

I knew he wanted to protect me, but I would have liked for him to show a little confidence in my ability to take care of myself. And for him to consider that I might actually be able to help.

He suggested I coach the Femmes in self-defense. Then he said I shouldn't stay with them. I should stick myself in the audience like a house plant.

I thought that by staying with the Femmes, I'd be in a great position to see or hear something unusual and alert Sam. I didn't plan to jump into the river. Things got out of hand.

What if our roles were reversed? Suppose I thought I knew where Sam was, then discovered he was unreachable. With a killer lurking. Suppose my communication with him was suddenly cut off. I would be terrified.

I had to stop testing the people I loved. Just because Lester rejected me, it didn't mean Sam would reject me.

Before we arranged this rendezvous, I promised Sam he could trust me. Now I had eluded his officer, disguised myself and disappeared despite his desire to protect me. I took a flying leap into the river toward danger and goaded my friends into leaping in with me.

And I couldn't take any of it back. It was too late. I'd blown it.

I put my head in my hands. How in the world could I possibly advise Buggy? I stared at the paper a long time before I began to write.

Dear Buggy,

Do some soul searching. You two love each other. Assure yourself and him of that all-important fact. Work on a plan to maintain your independence without eroding his trust. Have a powwow with him about specifics that bother you both. Talk them out. Work on a solution together that keeps you free and keeps him comfortable.

Sent with hope and love,
Aggie

I wished Buggy well. It was too late for me.

I clipped my pen on the pad and sank away from the light, back into the shadows. Completely invisible, I closed my eyes.

Minutes later, an elderly couple emerged from the shadows and approached the other end of the pool where it was shallow. While she watched, he walked down the steps and stood on the pool floor in waist-high water. He extended his hand up like a courtier to a queen. She stood straighter, making the lines in her neck disappear. Smiling, she stepped down two steps, placed her hand in his and slipped into the pool a step at a time, like royalty making a grand entrance. He watched her every move, his face filled with pleasure. I felt like I was I watching thc prelude to a dance.

When she reached him, they walked across the pool like players in a ritual, hands clasped under the water. They stepped to one side of the pool, back to the center, to the other side and back. They started across and back again with their opposite legs stepping sideways.

At the center of the pool, he turned his back to her, faced the deep end and took a step. She followed. He knew she was there, trusting him not to go deeper than she was able.

He maintained a slow, steady pace, confident she would keep up. He stayed within three feet of her, the length of her arms. The minute the water was deep enough to reach her neck, he turned to face her, and they stepped sideways in unison across the pool. An exercise? An eternal rhythm? A timeless dance? Occasionally, one of them smiled. They didn't touch but were only a reach away.

They arrived at the side of the pool where there was a waterfall. Holding hands, they stopped near the spray, threw their heads back and laughed, bouncing under shimmering particles. I closed my eyes and imagined their joyful mist spraying me.

When they walked back toward the steps, I waited for them to ascend. It didn't seem fitting to leave before they did.

Once they left, I took a deep breath and made my legs carry me to the lobby. The manager was there, apologizing to everyone within hearing distance.

He saw me and perked up. He leaned toward me conspiratorially and spoke in a low voice, "Ms. Mundeen. I'm happy to tell you the detective finally secured his penthouse, Suite 1205."

"Thank you. I'll be checking out."

Forty-Two

I entered the elevator and went up to five. When the door rolled open, a Hazmat officer faced me.

"The floor has just been cleared, miss. The rooms are fine."

"Thank you, officer."

I showered, washed and blew-dry my hair, dressed and packed my bag. Sighing, I plopped on the narrow bed beside my suitcase.

I sat there a long time before I stood, left the cubby hole and rolled my luggage to the elevator. Once inside, I punched a button. When the elevator stopped, I exited, strode slowly down the hall and knocked on a door.

The door to Suite 1205 opened. Sam stood there in a white t-shirt, khaki pants and socks with a hole in one toe.

"You're all right?" he said. "After your swim in the river?"

"I don't blame you for being angry. I was wrong."

"We've had this conversation."

"Yes. And you're furious."

He let out a sigh. "Why don't you come inside. We'll talk about it." He wedged the door open with my suitcase and gestured to the chairs and table across the room near the entrance to the balcony. The room was beautiful. Warm. I felt a chill. I sat. He sat across the table, hands clasped in his lap, and studied me.

"I'm sorry I ditched your policeman and went to dance with

the Femmes. I should have talked to you about it." He nodded. "Would you have agreed I should go with them instead of sitting in the audience?"

"Probably not. I'd have tried very hard to dissuade you."

At least he acknowledged we could have talked about it.

"I had a strong feeling I needed to be near them if the killer struck. Did you find out if Foxy, Phyllis or Martha smuggled drugs into the gift shop?"

"The DA says his office has a good case against the jailed suspects. They're sweating them to learn more about the cartel they work for. He cleared your friends."

"That's good."

"Yes. You can count on your friends. Now let's get back to whether I can count on you. When you decided to dance with the Femmes, you discounted our men backstage. You discounted me and the entire police force."

"I never meant to discount anyone. Especially the police." I hoped he believed me. "They wouldn't have jumped in the river, though."

"You're probably right about that. How did you know there were potassium cyanide crystals in that glass?"

"I didn't. I guessed. Once I examined the recessed fixtures and tunnel skylights in the storage closet and saw they had similar parts, I figured out the cyanide that killed the women could be placed in solid form inside the rims of the bathroom skylight above their heads."

"What storage closet?"

"Hall closets where maids keep supplies. I peeked in."

"Um, hmm. Go on."

"You told me that cyanide killed her," I said.

"Yes, but we didn't know cyanide could be changed into a gas until just before the parade. Or how it was delivered to the women. You could have shared that information."

"I hadn't figured it out. I did tell you about the skylights, remember? You were preoccupied with setting up surveillance on the river."

"That's right. I was."

"I kept seeing the girls' boyfriends with water bottles, sometimes with a lemon peel inside. I didn't make the connection to activating the crystals until I thought about what the man at the plating plant said about poison that looked like baking soda. Then I realized the barge driver looked familiar. I thought it was Roger Plunkett because of the medals on his chest. But they weren't perfectly lined up like he wore them. They were askew. When I saw him reach out to pour bottled water into the General's glass, it hit me. John Abbott was pouring acid water on potassium cyanide crystals to turn them into hydrogen cyanide gas."

"Abbott told us that when he climbed on the roof, he dumped potassium cyanide crystals down the solar light tunnel where they lay dormant inside the rim. When he knew the girls were primping in the most likely place in the bathroom, he poured in lemon water and slapped the cover on the roof before the acid worked. He knew if the gas couldn't escape upward, it would float down into the room."

"How did he know when the girls were primping?"

"He had a date with Monica, called her, told her he was on his way up and to make up her face and be beautiful."

"She'd already told him she'd decided to date only officers?"

"Yes. He was already depressed from receiving a general discharge. Her rejection was the last straw."

"John's father was a Major General who probably expected a lot of him. Why did he try to kill General Dayton?"

"He begged the General to change his discharge to honorable, but the General refused. When John started working for the plating company and realized he could steal small amounts of chemicals without being detected, he plotted to kill the General. He read up on what he needed and how to activate the crystals into a lethal gas. He stole a key to the supply closet, duplicated the key and hoarded chemicals, waiting for the right moment. When he'd stolen enough chemicals, he went to work for the roofing company.

"He started dating Monica when she stayed at the hotel. But she rejected him. When the company installed tunnel skylights, he realized he could put crystals inside the skylight tunnel where they'd lay dormant until he activated them. He read CPS was giving rebates to customers who installed solar systems and decided to open his own company where he'd be free to carry out his plan. When he saw his scheme worked on the women, he started thinking about where to kill the General. Roger Plunkett was ex-military and had connections to the river authority. So he was selected to drive the General's barge. John talked Roger into letting him drive it instead."

"Was Roger involved in the murders? Sara Giles saw two men enter and leave Monica's suite."

"John needed a buddy when he visited Monica. He needed to get into the bathroom and check the crystals in the skylight while Monica talked to Roger. Roger was unaware John planned to murder anybody."

"Why did John kill Sara?"

"She saw him and Roger come out of Monica's suite. John was afraid after Monica died, she'd name him as a suspect. He got to know her, called her for a date and played the same scenario with her."

"The man is really sick."

"Yes."

"Was he involved with the Day of the Dead pins and the smoke at NIOSA?"

"He combined Day of the Dead with Halloween and used

the dry ice smoke as a prank to cause chaos. He left skull pins near the bodies as an evil reminder that death was the fate of anybody who mistreated him."

"Why did he pin one on me?"

"He saw you getting close to the Femmes and wanted to scare you away. People and symbols were jumbled in John's mind."

"Who was the father of Monica's baby?"

"Hank Gleason. After we saved General Dayton, he was happy to be present when we questioned Major Gleason. Monica was out of the service when she and Gleason had their affair, so the Army can't charge him with a service-related offense. Now that the Army knows his history, I imagine Gleason will have a hard time getting promoted."

"Good. By the way, the man at Purely Plating told me his workers wear hazard suits, gloves and masks. They probably wear shoe covers, and John stole some."

"We found them in his apartment along with the shoes he wore. We also found a mask he asked Phyllis to get him from Nix Hospital. He told her he had allergies. We think the mask material will match fibers our evidence team found. He even snitched a chemical cartridge filter from the plating company and rigged it behind the mask to give him extra protection from the gas. John confessed, but it's good to have evidence."

"The man at Nix Hospital said their booties are flimsy and disintegrate in bad weather. They would have left traces on the carpet. So the killer got shoe covers somewhere else."

"You know the supply clerk at Nix Hospital?"

"I met him one day when I stopped in."

"Uh-huh. Did you snoop at the hospital before or after Detective Montaya went there?"

I looked out the window.

"After."

"That's what I figured."

"With so many people in town, they need more hospital gowns, booties and masks."

"You went up there posing as representative for a supply company?"

I nodded. "And I don't know how to get them the items they need."

He sighed. "I guess we'll have to find out who supplies the hospital so they can contact the Nix. Maybe Valerie will take care of that."

I turned sideways and admired the view so he couldn't see my pickled expression.

"Why didn't you tell me about the shoe covers at Purely Plating?"

"I just now thought of it. And you were always so busy, I didn't want to burden you with anything extra."

"Did it ever occur to you your meddling might interfere with our investigation and cost us more time?"

"No. I should have thought of that."

"Yes. You should have."

"You're furious with me, aren't you?"

"I love you, Aggie, but I have to make you understand. We discussed how I can't do my job and always be afraid for you. I know you want to help investigate. If you do, you have to share with me what you intend to do. I have to be able to trust you."

There it was. The whole problem. I wanted so much to participate in Sam's job, I didn't trust him enough to let him do it. When I flew off on my own and hid things, he couldn't trust me. We could never go in the same direction with one of us out of step.

"You think it's all right for me to help investigate as long as I share my findings with you?"

"Yes. If you don't interfere with the police investigation.

And tell me ahead of time what you're planning. Don't start sleuthing on your own where you put yourself in danger."

"I've gotten more careful about that."

"Except for your flying gaucho into the river."

We both grinned. "That was spontaneous. I can't give up spontaneity."

"I don't expect you to. It's one of the things I love about you." He leaned forward, chin on his fists like he did when he was most intent. "Tell me your ideas. We can devise a plan together. Can I trust you to do that?"

I looked at him dead on. "Yes."

"That way," he said, "I can keep you safe."

"You want to keep me. Safe."

We looked at each other across the table.

"Yes. I love you. I want you to trust me. And I need to be able to trust you."

"I do trust you, Sam. I always will. I promise. And I love you."

"We made those promises before. Can you be sure?"

Tears filled my eyes. "Yes. You can trust me. I understand now what it means. It was the dance."

He looked confused. "The Femmes' dance at Arneson Theater?"

"No. The one in the swimming pool. The permanence of it. The total trust."

He looked puzzled

"It's kind of hard to explain. I'll tell you later. Are you going to bring in my suitcase?"

He stood like a statue and studied me. "Are you sure you want me to bring it in? It's a big step."

I'd known him twenty years. I'd seen him in all kinds of situations. I loved everything about him.

I glanced over at the threshold. "Not too big."

He rolled my suitcase over the threshold, left it by the sofa and went back to lock the door.

When he walked toward me, I stood very still. He stopped and looked at me for a long time. Then he slowly nodded and drew me into his arms.

In case you missed the first book in the series

FIT TO BE DEAD (#1)

Aggie Mundeen, single and pushing forty, fears nothing but middle age. When she moves from Chicago to San Antonio, she knows she better shape up before anybody discovers she writes the column, "Stay Young with Aggie." She takes Aspects of Aging at University of the Holy Trinity and plunges into exercise at Fit and Firm.

Rusty at flirting and mechanically inept, she irritates a slew of male exercisers, then stumbles into murder. She'd like to impress the investigating detective with her sleuthing skills. But when the killer comes after her, the health club has to evacuate semi-clad patrons, the detective stalls his investigation, and Aggie forgoes fitness to try to stay alive.

Lefty Award Finalist for Best Humorous Mystery

"Fit to Be Dead has intriguing characters that point to romance, an engrossing plot and well-disguised clues —a fun read."__L. C. Hayden, Award Winning Author of the Harry Bronson Mystery series.

Second Edition

In case you missed the second book in the series

DANG NEAR DEAD (#2)

Aggie vacations with Sam and Meridith at a Texas Hill Country dude ranch. She will advise her column readers on how to stay young and fresh in summer. Except for wanglers, heat, snakes and poison ivy, what could go wrong?

The manager is jealous of her assistant, the former ranch owners died suspiciously, and wranglers hold secrets about the ranch. When an expert rider flies off a horse and lies in a coma, Aggie is convinced somebody caused the fall and is determined to expose the assailant. She encounters a cabal of cowboys and learns that more than one hombre in the bunch would like to see her *permanently* home on the range.

Mystery Finalist-International Chanticleer Award

"Aggie does it again. ...I love this character. Nancy West does such a good job of making Aggie humorous, but with a brain." __Jeniffer Gott, Houston Reviewer

Second Edition

In case you missed the third book in the series

SMART, BUT DEAD (#3

Skirting forty and appalled by the prospect of slip-sliding into middle-age, Aggie blasts off to the local university to study the genetics of aging . She is doggedly determined to stay young.

Despite conflicts with her professor, she learns about genetics and DNA. When she discovers a dead body, the San Antonio detective urges her to avoid the investigation. But dangerously curious , she races to solve the crime, winds up prime suspect and is on target to become next campus corpse.

With two brilliant women scientists awarded the 2020 Novel Prize in Chemistry for discovering a gene-editing tool, this is a timely mystery.

MYSTERY FINALIST- CHANTICLEER AWARD

"Smart, But Dead is funny, yet intriguing, West's humorous Aggie Mundeen Mysteries are the best I have read. "

Second Edition

Nancy G. West

Originally a business major, Nancy discovered that writing stories was a lot more fun than accounting. She is writing book two of the spin-off series, Aggie Mundeen's Lake Mysteries, and recently completed a suspense novel for adults and teens. She lives with her family in San Antonio, the setting for *River City Dead*.

VISIT THE AUTHOR

Website

www.nancygwest.com

Special offers, updates and author insights

https://www.subscribepage.com/a1n3n1

Aggie Blogs About Her Author

https://bit.ly/3dhwMrD

Facebook

Facebook.com/authorNancyG.West